Praise for

THE GUY WHO PUMPS
YOUR GAS HATES YOU

"An incisive evocation of your average aimless twenty-
something Winnipeg male's unfocused yearning for, well,
anything beyond the next cheap beer. Sean Trinder's
sharp-witted depiction of the vast psychological mindscape
between juvenile apathy and adult identity hit me like a gust
of February wind at Portage and Main."

— Corey Redekop
Author, *Husk* and *Shelf Monkey*

"Sean Trinder writes so well I want to punch him in the
face. *The Guy Who Pumps Your Gas Hates You* is full of
beer, cigarettes, joints, music, driving, dead-end jobs,
relationships, friendships, emotions, dreams, and broken
hearts. I don't know that I've ever read the suburban working
Canadian life I grew up in written about so well."

—TJ Dawe
Playwright, *Dishpig* and *The Slipknot*

 **NUNATAK FICTION**

Nunatak is an Inuktitut word meaning "lonely peak," a rock or mountain rising above ice. During Quaternary glaciation in North America these peaks stood above the ice sheet and so became refuges for plant and animal life. Magnificent nunataks, their bases scoured by glaciers, can be seen along the Highwood Pass in the Alberta Rocky Mountains and on Ellesmere Island.

Newest Press' Nunatak First Fiction Series are specially selected works of outstanding fiction by new western writers.

THE GUY A NOVEL
WHO PUMPS
YOUR GAS
HATES YOU

BY SEAN TRINDER

NeWest
PRESS

COPYRIGHT © SEAN TRINDER 2015

— — —

Library and Archives Canada Cataloguing in Publication

Trinder, Sean, 1981-
     The guy who pumps your gas hates you / Sean Trinder.

(Nunatak first fiction series : 39) Issued in print and electronic formats. ISBN 978-1-927063-78-1 (pbk.).--ISBN 978-1-927063-79-8 (epub).-- ISBN 978-1-927063-80-4 (mobi)

     I. The guy who pumps your gas hates you. II. Series: Nunatak first fiction ; 39

PS8639.R57G89 2015   C813'.6   C2014-906468-3   C2014-906469-1

— — —

Editor For the Board: Leslie Vermeer
Cover & Interior Design: Greg Vickers
Cover Photography: Barb Dubrawski
Author Photo: Lindsay Winter, Lindsay Winter Photography

NeWest Press acknowledges the financial support of the Alberta Multimedia Development Fund and the Edmonton Arts Council for our publishing program. We further acknowledge the financial support of the Government of Canada through the Canada Book Fund (CBF) for our publishing activities. We acknowledge the support of the Canada Council for the Arts, which last year invested $24.3 million in writing and publishing throughout Canada.

201, 8540–109 Street
Edmonton, Alberta | T6G 1E6
780.432.9427
www.newestpress.com

NeWest Press

No bison were harmed in the making of this book.

We are committed to protecting the environment and to the responsible use of natural resources. This book was printed on 100% post-consumer recycled paper.

Printed in Canada

For my parents ...

... for being nothing like the parents in this book.

CHAPTER 01

The customer is always right. Always. They have to be. For their own protection. More than they are always entitled, more than they are always ignorant and always arrogant, they are always right, and this almost divine infallibility is the only thing keeping them from getting the pointy end of a pen stabbed through the eye. Because it would be wrong to stab the eyes of customers. Because we are wrong and by some sort of cosmic injustice they are always right. Always.

But that's all bullshit. Whether you pump gas or serve tables in a restaurant or you're a teller in a bank or whatever fucking customer service job you may have, at some point some manager or supervisor or dick boss will come up to you and utter the biggest lie in the history of work and lies.

"Remember," the manager'll say, "the customer is always right." Which translated means, "Those people lining up for [insert whatever the fuck you're selling], they make me money. You cost me money. You're shit and they're gods. Treat them accordingly."

That's essentially it.

And you know it was some shitty manager who thought up this shitty mantra, 'cause he doesn't give a fuck. He's not a grunt on the front lines fending off the public while fighting homicidal pen-stabby urges. He's in the back office pretending to go over paperwork while surfing Internet porn. The only time he has to deal with customers is when you finally lose it and actually do stab someone in the eye. Then he comes out and smoothes everything over with some fifty-percent-off coupons, and you're looking for a new job.

Fucking prick.

The mantra is bullshit. The fact that someone had to think it up in the first place proves just how bullshit it is. Ben Affleck very eloquently stated the truth in the American cinematic classic *Mallrats*. "The customer is always an asshole," he said. So true. That's my mantra. They're all assholes, every last one of them. Even when they're not outwardly being assholes, they're assholes. It's just easier to think this way. It makes work and life livable.

I've been pumping gas for three years. I'm good at it, which is sad. No one should ever work at a gas station long enough to get good at it. You should work there for only a few months in high school, then move the fuck on. I didn't. I started when I was seventeen at a Shell station on Dakota, across from St. Vital Mall. Our proximity to the mall and to the Perimeter Highway, and the fact that we were the only place for miles that sold diesel, ensured that we were busy as fuck all the fucking time. I quickly learned that being fast was an asset. I worked there until, when I was eighteen, I was arrested for drinking and driving and I lost my licence. I was forced to find a job closer to home in Oakbank that I could walk to, and since my only experience was pumping gas, the only job I could find was at a gas station/hardware store on Oakbank's main drag. My bosses there were a middle-aged couple. They were both schizophrenic. Not clinically, but they acted like it. One day they'd be your best friend, and the next they'd be bitching you out for something stupid for no reason at all. You can only take so much of that kind of instability, so eventually I applied at the CountryGas gas station across the street and got hired on there. Quitting the hardware store was one of the most satisfying things I've ever done.

Fast forward one year and I'm twenty years old and still at the CountryGas station, and my total work experience is still just pumping liquefied dinosaur bones into the tanks of people's shitty cars. It's not my fault I'm in this rut. Staying at this gas station is just too easy. The customers suck, sure, but my boss, Jane, is a sweetheart and for the most part the people I work with are pretty great. So, other than this powerful feeling that my future is getting bleaker and bleaker with every day I unintentionally huff gas fumes, I'm content.

More or less.

I'm at the gas station now, working the evening shift, 6:00 to 11:00 p.m. It's ten thirty and I'm rinsing out the coffee jugs in the sink in the back bathroom. I'm working with Heidi. She's up at the front manning (or womanning) the store while I get ready for close. Normally I work the morning shift, six to noon, with a guy named Shane, but Erica (another girl we work with) wanted my morning shift so that she could have this evening free, so we switched. I'm just now realizing how stupid that was on my part. I won't be home till at least eleven thirty, and then I'll be up at five o'clock tomorrow to come open the store with Shane. I'm going to be tired as shit. This is the last time I help out a co-worker. Helping people always ends badly for me.

I'm shaken out of my moment of self-pity by Heidi calling to me from the front counter.

"Brendan," she says, "make yourself scarce."

I know what this means. I grumble the word *fuck* and duck out of the bathroom and into the back, into Jane's little office with the two-way mirror above her desk. Through the mirror I have a straight-on view of the counter where Heidi is helping a young blonde asshole customer who has just walked in. I can see them but they can't see me. That's how two-way mirrors work, in case you've never seen a fucking cop show on TV.

The blonde asshole customer is my ex-girlfriend, Marissa, although to imply that we were actually in any sort of traditional relationship is misleading. I thought we were, because that's what you think when you go out drinking with a girl every weekend and then go back to her place sometimes to have sex. But I guess I'm just traditional. Marissa was not, evidenced by the fact that she was fucking other guys while we were "together." And really, there's nothing wrong with that. This is the twenty-first century. If a girl wants to have sex with any willing party, that's her business. It would just be nice if the girl were honest with all parties involved, instead of letting one of the parties (me) find out from Erica at work that said girl was all over some dude at Buffalo Bills nightclub when said girl said she was going to be home studying.

While I respect a woman's desire to be free and unencumbered, I myself am strictly monogamous. The idea of having multiple partners freaks me out. That's how diseases get spread, am I right? I like to be with one girl, and it's my desire that when I'm with that one girl, she's with only one guy: me. After Erica told me what was going on, as soon as I got home from work, I called Marissa up and got her to spill, and that was the last I've spoken to her.

Well, kind of.

Marissa keeps showing up at the gas station. It's the damnedest fucking thing. She keeps showing up like everything's cool, like nothing shitty happened. She gets gas, she gets a bag of chips or whatever, she asks me how I'm doing and she leaves. Like, what the fuck? Aren't there other gas stations in the world? Fuck off.

And just as I think it, Marissa fucks off. She turns from the counter and walks out the door, leaving Heidi alone at the front. I exit the office, grab the coffee jugs from the bathroom sink and set them back in their holders on the red counter that runs along the wall beside our big cashout counter with the tills on it. I rejoin Heidi.

"I fucking hate her," she says, referring undoubtedly to Marissa.

"You and me both," I say. "Thanks for the heads up."

"Aren't there other gas stations she can go to?" Heidi asks.

I laugh.

"I was just thinking that," I say.

Heidi looks Asian. She's actually Ukrainian, I think, but she looks Asian. She doesn't have the eyes, but she's short and skinny and she's got long, straight black hair. She's a straight edge. She doesn't smoke, doesn't drink and strongly dislikes those who do in her presence. I refrain from smoking when I work with her to stay on her good side. I like Heidi. Of all the girls who work at the CountryGas station, she's my favourite by far. She's idealistic, and since my cynicism is just soured idealism, we're compatible as friends. I don't have any siblings, but if I could choose a younger sister, I'd choose Heidi.

Sure, she hates smokers and I'm a smoker, and she hates drunks and I spend most of my weekend nights getting shitfaced, but we share a mutual love of music and that's enough to build a friendship on.

She's got a CD playing in the little CD player/radio by the window to our right. What's coming out of it sounds good.

"That sounds good," I say. "What are we listening to?"

"Ben Kweller," she says. "You like?"

"It's good."

"You want me to burn you a CD?"

"Nah, that's cool."

"You still doing your cleanse?"

"Yeah."

"Well, tell me when you wanna do a binge, 'cause I got a lotta stuff you should hear," Heidi says.

"Sounds good," I say.

I should explain my cleanse. From grades seven to ten, I listened to punk rock. That's really how I became addicted to music, through punk rock. I'd heard the Clash and the Ramones and the Pretenders on the radio before, but it never occurred to me that that was punk. I thought it was just radio music, stuff that never really pertained to me. Then I heard Green Day and the Offspring and that's when things changed. That was the first needle in the arm, so to speak. Music was no longer something that just played in the background of my life. I was a junkie, and punk rock was my heroin. That first fix led me to more underground bands like Pennywise, NOFX, Descendants, Guy Smiley, Lagwagon, Sick of It All, etc., etc. I even formed a punk band with some friends. We'd play all ages shows at Ozzy's and the Park Theatre in Osborne Village. It was fun.

In tenth grade, about the time my band broke up, I found that punk just wasn't heavy enough for me anymore. Enter Pantera, Megadeth, Fear Factory, Machine Head, Nothingface and even some of the Nu Metal shit like

Rage Against the Machine, Snot and System of a Down. Metal owned me for the rest of my school days. It matched my shitty outlook on life. Then I graduated. Then my outlook on life wasn't so shitty. It was still a little shitty, but not as shitty as when I was stuck in school. Suddenly, my metal albums weren't doing it for me. I was a music lover without a genre to own.

It was around this unsatisfying time that the movie *Good Will Hunting* entered my life. I loved that movie. Still do. I must've rented it three times from the video store beside the CountryGas station before I finally bought it. One of the many amazing things about the movie was the soundtrack, particularly the soft, delicate acoustic songs that augmented the dramatic scenes they appeared in. A quick scan of the end credits informed me that these songs were performed by a man named Elliott Smith.

I found his disc *Either/Or* at a second-hand music store in Transcona. One listen was like that first musical fix all over again. Those simple, acoustic-guitar-driven songs reminded me why I was an addict and why I could never go clean. It was songwriting at its simplest and most wonderful. This shit was the shit.

I ignored the rest of my sizeable CD collection and went on a hunt. I scoured every small independent record store in Winnipeg looking for Elliott Smith discs. Some were easier to find than others, but eventually I had them all: the self-titled one, *Figure 8*, *Roman Candle*, *XO*. These became my CD collection. I'd turn on my stereo and ask not, "What CD am I going to listen to?" but rather, "What Elliott Smith disc am I going to listen to?" It was Elliott or it was nothing.

Hence, the cleanse.

It's eleven o'clock. I switch off the open sign and go outside to take the pump readings. Once back inside I write down the readings from the dip machine and call them in to the trucking company that delivers our gas. Then Heidi and I cash out the tills. With that done and all the printouts together and on Jane's desk, Heidi and I turn out the lights, lock the door and leave.

Heidi offers me a ride home, but I decline. I haven't had a cigarette in hours and I'm quite certain she won't let me spark one up in her car. So she drives off and I light an Export Gold and I start my twenty-minute walk home. I take my Discman out of my backpack. I put the headphones on and hit play. *XO* starts and I smile.

The gas station is located in a strip mall that was built when I was just a little kid. I remember when it first opened. My friends and I would collect all the nickels and dimes and quarters we could find, and we'd go there to buy candy. We'd get together afterwards at whoever's house and gorge ourselves on Popeye Cigarettes, Mackintosh Toffee, chocolate bars, chips and pop. A few years later,

I'd get my allowance from my dad and I'd walk to the gas station to buy comic books. I'd spend all my money on fantastic stories of adventure and mayhem and be broke for the rest of the month until I'd get my allowance again at the beginning of the next month — coincidentally when new comics would come out. And a few years after that, I would buy cigarettes at the gas station, fooling the teenage clerks by looking older than my years.

It seems fitting that I now work at CountryGas. It has been a part of my life just as much as any friend I've ever had.

When I get home, I can hear my dad snoring. I brush my teeth and then I'm in bed, too. Less than six hours till I'm back at work. Awesome.

I close my eyes.

That was Monday, September 10, 2001. As I sleep, the bubble that has isolated North America from the rest of the world is still fully intact. Universality is still a foreign concept to us. Up until this very point in time, the United States and Canada have been joyfully kicking ass and taking names throughout the world with next to no domestic repercussions. That will all end tomorrow. Tomorrow, the bubble will pop, thanks to a small group of men armed only with box cutters.

But I'm getting a little ahead of myself.

CHAPTER 02

"Two planes just flew into the World Trade Center."

I stand looking at the asshole customer on the other side of the counter from me. I'm tired. I can't tell if he's full of shit or not. You get a lot of bullshit info from customers when you work in a gas station. One time a guy came in telling me there was a pileup down the highway just out of town. I asked him how many cars were involved. He told me two. I politely explained to him that a two-car pileup isn't a pileup. It's an accident.

"What do you mean two planes flew into the World Trade Center?" I say. "Like, at the same time?"

"That's just really bad air traffic controlling," Shane says beside me.

"It's on the radio," the customer says. "They're saying it's a terrorist attack."

"Who's saying that?"

"The radio."

"How does the radio know that?"

"How big were the planes?" I ask.

"Big planes. Like commercial jets."

"Fuck off."

"That's what they're saying. Turn on your radio."

So we did and the radio told us exactly what the customer was saying. Planes had flown into the north and south towers of the World Trade Center. The US government says the planes were hijacked by terrorists. Around nine thirty, the radio tells us another plane crashed into the Pentagon. Emergency personnel were scrambling at the attack sites to save all they could. Basically, shit was hitting the fan down south.

Jane usually shows up at the gas station at about ten thirty. Today she doesn't. She calls and tells us that she can't leave the house. She's glued to CNN. She tells us there's video of the second plane hitting the tower. She tells us it's just awful.

Shane hangs up the phone.

"Should we do some sort of promotion today?" he asks me.

"Like what?"

"I don't know. Fifty percent off windshield washer fluid for Terrorist Tuesday?"

I laugh. It's nice working with someone who has as dark a sense of humour as your own. Safe people and people who can find a joke in a terrorist attack don't often get along.

Once our shift ended and I was home, though, I couldn't find anything very funny in what I was watching on the news. When it showed the second plane slamming into the tower, it felt like a bat hit me in the gut. How many people? Probably about one hundred, all killed in an instant. And that was just the people on the plane. How many people were in that building? How many watched helplessly as that plane came at them? Jesus fucking Christ.

The news tells me that both towers have fallen. There's video of them going down, people running and hiding from the resulting tidal wave of dust. I turn off the TV. I've had enough. It's all so terrible.

Normally, after a morning shift, when I get home I nap for a few hours, but I don't feel like it today, so I brew some coffee and make myself a sandwich. By four o'clock, my dad is home.

"You ready to go to war?" he asks me when he comes through the door.

"Huh?"

"We were attacked today," he says, setting down his tool bag. "Don't tell me you've been fucking sleeping all day. Haven't you seen the news?"

"I didn't hear that Canada was attacked," I say.

"Our ally was attacked. That means we were attacked just the same. When your buddies are down, you come in and help them out," my dad says.

"So who are we going to war against?" I ask.

"The fucking Arabs, who d'you think?" he says.

My dad pronounces it *A*-rabs, same as most old racists do. He's a bricklayer in his fifties and has the narrow worldview that most blue-collar assholes born in the '50s share. My mother left us when I was nine years old, mainly, I think, because my dear old dad is incredibly unpleasant to be around. She lives back in Toronto now. She sends me money sometimes.

My dad sits at the kitchen table with me.

"Me and your mom were in an airport once. This was before you were born. Security was talking to this Arab family. It was a man and his wife and a little kid. Security was talking to the man and out of nowhere he pulls out a knife and starts waving it around. Security took him down like that. They drag him away and he's screaming in his fucked-up language. They're violent people, those sand niggers. Their entire religion is based around violence. I have no doubt in my mind it was the Arabs who hijacked those planes," my dad says.

Silence. My dad just now notices the hotdogs and Kraft Dinner I've made for dinner.

"Kraft Dinner again? Christ. Can't you make anything else?" he asks.

"That guy in the airport ..."

"Yeah?"

"You ever think he might have just been scared?" I ask.

"What do you mean?"

"Well, he's in a different country, probably a different continent, and he's in an airport being threatened by security. He's got his family with him and he's afraid for them. He doesn't want anything bad to happen to them, he's got his back to the wall, so he pulls his knife 'cause that's all he's got. I'd do the same thing in his position. You would, too," I say.

My dad is scooping cheesy noodles onto the plate I set out for him.

"If security was talking to him, they had a reason. Fuck him," he says.

He stands with his plate of food, grabs a bottle of beer from the fridge and heads into the living room, leaving me to eat in the kitchen alone.

CHAPTER 03

"Um, I was here first."

I look up from where I'm ringing through a gas purchase for a tall woman with short blonde hair. There's a middle-aged woman behind her who's holding up her hand to gain my attention.

"I'm sorry?" I say.

The middle-aged woman steps up to the counter, beside the tall woman with the short hair.

"I was here first," she says. "This woman came in after me. You should be serving me first. It's only fair."

I glance out the window to my right. Shane is still filling the middle-aged woman's van.

"I'm sorry, ma'am, but that's not how we do things," I say.

"This woman's gas is done, so I'm ringing her through so she can get on with her day. When your gas is done, I'll do the same for you."

The blonde woman looks embarrassed for everyone.

"No," the middle-aged woman says. "That's unacceptable. I was here first, I should be served first. It's only fair."

I give the blonde woman her receipt and she's out the door and into her Geo Metro.

"I don't know what to tell you, lady," I say.

The two of us stand in tense silence until Shane finishes her fill. I check the amount on the machine under the window.

"Your gas is done," I say.

"Oh, is it my turn now?"

"Yes."

"Lucky me."

Shane comes back inside while I'm ringing through the middle-aged bitch's purchase. He sees me give her back the finger when she leaves.

"What's all this?" Shane asks.

"Nothing. She was a bitch," I say.

"Cool," he says. "You coming to the bar tonight? Chase the Ace is up to thirteen hundred bucks."

"Can't tonight. I've got my thing."

"What thing?"

"My class."

"Your writing class?"

"Yeah."

"You're still doing that?"

"I've had one class so far. Yeah, I'm still doing that."

I should explain. I love writing. Always have. I've been writing stories since I was a kid, probably since I learned how to write. I can't explain the attraction, really. I've just always loved putting words together into sentences, sentences into paragraphs, paragraphs into pages. Some people knit, others play piano, I write stories.

When I was eighteen, I wrote a novel. It was the first really serious thing I'd ever written. It was 1999 and Columbine had just happened. I was watching Oprah, and Oprah had on the mother of one of the victims and the mother was talking about her crusade to end gun violence. I remember watching this and feeling really bummed out. I remember thinking that, had I been killed in a school shooting, I'd want my mother to carry on with her life and not be constantly reminded of the horrific way in which I expired.

I started writing my novel the next day. I was inspired. I wrote about a young man who survives a shooting in his school. I wrote about everything that happens to him as a result, as he attempts to mend his wounds, both physical and spiritual. It took me a year to finish it and I was very proud of the end product. I printed out copies for my friends to read, and the feedback was overwhelmingly positive. I sent out some queries to Canadian book publishers and started collecting rejection letters.

After what happened with Marissa, I wasn't feeling too great about myself. My sense of self-worth wasn't fucking great, let's say. I was upset about my station in life, that I was twenty and pumping gas and no girls want guys who are twenty and still work pumping gas. I remember asking myself, "What do you want to be?" The answer was easy. I wanted to be a novelist. More than anything in the world.

So I pulled myself up and went to the University of Winnipeg, and I signed up for an Advanced Creative Writing class offered through Continuing Education. It was a first step, and it beat the hell out of self-loathing. My first class was last week.

And so, after my shift was over, I walked home, had a nap, got up, made dinner for my dad and me and at six o'clock I was in my shitty little Mazda B2000 truck with my notebook, heading into the city.

I park my shitty truck on Portage, just a little way down from the Continuing Education building. It's after five thirty, so I park for free, which is good 'cause I have no change on me. I light a cigarette as I walk, and I just hang out outside the doors of the building while I finish it. Then I'm in the building and up the stairs to our room.

It was established last week that this course would be more of a writing-workshop kind of thing. Our professor, Kate, explained that we already knew how to write, obviously, so there was no point in her standing before us, telling us how to write well, 'cause what does that even mean, anyway. So starting today, we'd all gather together and share our writing and constructively evaluate each other. I've never really read any of my creative writing aloud to anyone before, so right now I'm scared shitless. And a little excited.

The tables in the room are arranged in a giant rectangle so that when we're seated we're all facing one another, sort of. I sit. Most of the other writers are already here. I'm the youngest by far. Most are middle aged, save for one woman who sits directly across from me. She's maybe in her late twenties or thirty. She looks artsy. She wears all black. She could be a witch.

The man to my left is in a wheelchair. Last week he told me he's writing a novel about his accident, how he ended up becoming paralyzed. I didn't know what to say to that, so I said, "Good for you," which I now know sounds condescending as all hell. But what was I supposed to say?

The woman who sits to my right looks like a hippie. I imagine her works will all be about sun goddesses and flower children and the curse of menopause, or whatever.

Kate arrives and takes a seat at the rectangle table. When she's satisfied all the wannabe writers are here, she stands again.

"Good to see you all back," she says. "So, today's the big day. Who'd like to go first?"

Silence. Everyone is staring down at the table in front of themselves. I wait until I'm sure no one will volunteer, and then I raise my hand. Kate sees it and smiles.

"Go ahead, Brendan."

I open my notebook and clear my throat.

"This is a poem I wrote recently. I hope you like it," I say.

The poem goes like so:

Four walls and a bed and a song in my head
about a shell on a sandy beach.
One shell in a hundred and empty as it started
when it washed up on the land that it reached.
Alone among many and beautiful as the next.
What a mess. All are left.
A ceiling above me and a flower who loves me
as she did when I cut her stem.
One rose alone with me, still at home with me
where she'll grow to be beautiful again.
And I'll be here with her long after she wilts.
What a sight. Nice as night.

I close my notebook. It takes a while for me to look up, but when I do, my fellow writers are smiling at me.

"That was really nice," the guy in the wheelchair says.

The hippie pats my shoulder and says, "Good job."

I don't get a lot of positive reinforcement at work. And my dad is a complete dick. I spend most of my time getting shit on. This little bit of encouragement for something I feel strongly about means the whole fucking world to me. I could cry. Instead I grin like an idiot while others read the shit they brought. At eight o'clock, we stop for a fifteen-minute break. I head outside and light up an Export Gold. I lean against the building. The sky to the east is getting dark. The sun is almost setting in the west. The days are getting shorter. It'll be fall soon, then winter. I'm not looking forward to it. Pumping gas sucks in winter.

I'm smoking and watching the cars go by on Portage. I don't notice the witch approach me.

"You got a light?" she asks me.

She puts a cigarette between her lips and I cup my lighter to the end of it. She exhales a smooth jet trail of smoke.

"Thanks, man," she says. "I liked your poem."

"Thanks."

"My name's Anne," Anne says and holds out her hand to mine. I shake it.

"I'm Brendan," I say. "What's with all the black, Anne?"

"I'm a big Johnny Cash fan. How old are you, Brendan?"

"I'm twenty."

"You look older than that."

"I've done a lot of hard living."

"Who hasn't?"

"How old are you, Anne?"

"I'm twenty-seven."

"You look younger than that."

Anne looks at me like I've insulted her. Then she says, "You're sweet."

We stand smoking in silence for a moment. I drop my butt to the sidewalk and crush it out under my shoe.

"We should probably head back up," I say.

Anne is looking past me. She points down the street.

"You ever go there?" she asks.

I turn and follow her pointed finger with my eyes to a little café.

"Can't say that I do," I say.

"After class, you wanna go have coffee with me?" she asks.

"Sure," I say, a little too quickly and a little too enthusiastically.

"Great," Anne says. "We should probably head back up."

"Right."

Anne crushes out her butt, and we're up the stairs and back in our room. In our last hour, those who haven't shared share. When it's Anne's turn, she reads a short story about a woman confronting a sexist co-worker. She uses the word *fuck* a lot. I like that. I like foul-mouthed people. Anne doesn't look at me once until the end of class. As I gather up my notebook, she walks over to me and says, "Let's go."

We walk to the café and sit in a booth. The waitress takes our order. I ask for a coffee and Anne asks for a black coffee. I'm not surprised.

"This place is kinda nice," I say, looking around. "You come here a lot?"

"What was your poem about?" Anne asks.

I stare at her for a moment, and she stares back at me. Anne has a monotone directness that throws me off. Women my age aren't like her.

I groan.

"I wrote that poem one night when I was drunk. I came home from the bar and I wrote it. I always feel really alone at the bar, which is fucked 'cause my friends are there and I'm surrounded by people and the women are all 'beautiful,' but honestly I fucking hate it there. I really want a girlfriend but I know I'll never find one at the bar, which sucks 'cause I'm twenty and the only fucking thing to do when you're twenty is go to the fucking bar."

"So stop going to the bar," Anne says.

"Okay."

"Or don't and be miserable."

"Miserable I understand."

"It's your life."

"Why are you miserable?"

"Am I miserable?"

"I don't know. Are you a witch?"

Anne sits up straight and smiles at me, a genuine smile. The waitress comes and drops off our coffees. When she leaves, Anne lights a cigarette.

"Since the beginning of time, men have tried to subjugate women when they realize their power. Strong women were killed for being strong by weak, fearful men. From the shackles of man-made prisons, witches rise. Witches are women who could not be conquered," Anne says.

I'm stirring cream into my coffee.

"So, are you a witch?" I ask.

Anne ashes her cigarette.

"No. But I'd like to be," she says.

CHAPTER 04

I have a favourite asshole customer. He comes in every morning right at six. He gets a large coffee cup, fills it half full with coffee and then goes to the bathroom and fills it the rest of the way with cold water. He brings it to the counter, makes a comment about how our coffee is too hot, then demands to be charged only half price, 'cause half of his coffee is just water. And we oblige him, because he's an idiot. But he isn't, though. He's a car mechanic. He owns a shop down Oakbank's main street. Every day he fixes cars. That's not exactly moron work. Yet this same asshole can't figure out that if you just wait two minutes, your hot coffee will cool down.

Amazing.

Later in my shift, I'm selling cigarettes to a blonde woman with an unnatural tan. After money passes from her to me and I give her her pack, she kind of lingers at the counter. There's no one else in the store.

"I was diagnosed with cancer two years ago," she tells me for some reason.

"Oh shit," I say.

"Yeah, oh shit," she says. "Breast cancer. I'm fine now, but you know what the first thing I did was after the doctor told me?"

"No. What?"

"I bought my first pack of cigarettes. Fuck it, right?" she said.

I laugh and so does she. She puts her cigarettes in her purse and leaves. Shane comes in from pumping gas right after she disappears.

"Mind if I step out for a smoke?" I ask him.

It's dead so he says, "Go nuts."

Today is Friday. When my shift ends, I walk home smoking cigarettes, then nap, get up, shower, eat some food. At exactly six o'clock my friend George's Chevy Blazer arrives in the driveway. I can hear his stereo from inside my house. Outside it's infinitely louder. I hop into the passenger seat and George greets me with a *Hey, buddy*. We hit the vendor and buy a couple of two-fours, and then we're heading into the city. George has *Far*

Beyond Driven on his stereo. The entire way to the city, he's drumming along to Vinnie Paul on his steering wheel.

I met George in junior high when I was playing in a band. George was playing drums in a death metal band that we'd share the bill with once in a while. We learned that George was also from Oakbank, and when our first drummer quit on us, we convinced George to replace him. He's been one of my best friends ever since. When I lost my licence, George would show up at my house every Friday at six o'clock and we'd get cases of beer and bomb it into the city. I now have my licence back, but that tradition continues. Basically, George is a stand-up motherfucker.

He now plays drums in a band called Lost Astronaut with the guitarist from my old band, Davis, and two younger guys Davis and I went to high school with, Marc (singer) and Jonas (bass). Jonas's mom is single and spends the weekends at her boyfriend's place, so Jonas's house becomes party central. We pre-game there, then head to the Oak nightclub and continue drinking, then back to Jonas's to pass out. Aside from the nightclub part, it's a lot of fun.

When we arrive at Jonas's place, Jonas, Davis and Marc are sitting around the kitchen table, drinking. George and I join them.

"'Dr. Feelgood' has the best opening of any rock song ever," Marc is saying.

"No way, man. 'Strength Beyond Strength,'" from George.

"Are we counting the Beatles as rock?" Davis asks.

"No," from Jonas.

This is how typical conversations go. These four talk about music more than anyone I know — even Heidi, and she lives for music. My friends are certain they're going to become rock stars. There's no doubt in their minds. The problem is, they spend more time drinking in bars than performing in bars.

We pound beers in Jonas's kitchen until about ten o'clock. Then we call a cab and the cab takes us to the Oak where we wait in line for twenty minutes before we're let in. I'm useless in the bar. I'm not terribly good looking. I'm certainly not ugly, but I'm not the kind of guy a girl sees and absolutely must fuck. I think my sense of humour redeems me, but when you can't talk 'cause the music's too loud, a great sense of humour doesn't count for shit. So I spend my time in the bar getting drunker and drunker, listening to music I don't like and glancing at girls I'm not overly attracted to anyway.

At two when the lights come on, I stumble outside to regroup with the others in the parking lot. I can't spot them, so I lean up against the wall of the club. Amy approaches me from nowhere.

"Hi, Brendan," she says.

"Hey, Amy," I say. "How're you?"

"I'm good. You look pretty drunk."

"Yeah."

"Still drinking lots."

"Yeah."

"Well, you take care of yourself, Brendan," she says, and she walks away and disappears into the sea of drunk people.

I'm instantly bummed out. Seeing Amy reminds me of a very bad thing I did the summer I turned eighteen. My friend from high school, Kyle, collected money from people and rented the overflow campground at Birds Hill Park. A shit-ton of us camped and partied for an entire weekend. The first night of camping was kind of a blur. I drank a twelve and smoked a bunch of dope in a tent with two girls. I was pretty lit up. Amy was there, and at one point in the night she asked me if I'd walk her to the bathroom, and I did. I waited for her outside and we walked back towards the campground. We were walking arm in arm and her boob was resting on me. In my messed-up state, I took this as an invitation to stick my hand up her shirt and grab her boob. Amy stopped walking. She froze.

"I knew this would happen," she said.

I removed my hand from her shirt.

"You wanna go back to the campsite?" I asked.

"Yes," she said.

And we did.

I've seen Amy around several times since this happened two years ago, but we've never discussed it. I want to apologize for molesting her, but how do you do that? How do you make amends for that?

I suck. No wonder Marissa cheated on me. I deserve much worse.

CHAPTER 05

I wake up on Jonas's living room floor. I stand up, walk into the bathroom, kneel down at the toilet and throw up. When that's done, I go into the kitchen and drink my weight in water. When I'm done with that, I go into the garage and light a cigarette. George is there. He's smoking too.

"Fun night last night," he says.

"Yeah," I lie.

"You hungry?"

"No. I just threw up."

"You wanna watch me eat breakfast?"

"Sure. Where?"

"Perkins?"

"Cool."

We go outside, get into George's truck and roll out.

After breakfast, George drops me off at home. I sleep some more until my dad wakes me up at one o'clock, telling me I'm wasting my life. I sit at the desk in my room and write in a notebook until the afternoon becomes evening. I get into my truck and head to the bank and take out some money from the ATM. As I'm walking back to my truck, a much bigger truck pulls into the parking lot. Ratboy is in the passenger seat. A guy I don't really know is driving.

"Hey, Brendan," Ratboy says. "How's it going?"

"Not bad."

"What're you up to tonight?" he asks.

"No plans, man."

"We're heading to a house party in the sticks. Wanna come?"

"Sure."

"Hop in."

And I do. I leave my truck in the bank parking lot and I climb in next to Ratboy. Ratboy is a friend of my old friend Kyle. I've known him since high school. We call him Ratboy because he's small and his nose is long and pointy, like a rat's.

The house party is full of people I only sort of recognize from working at CountryGas. I don't have any strong ties to Oakbank. I've lived there all my life, but I went to school in the city, in Transcona. The majority of my friends live in the city. Most people from Oakbank, I don't know. This is a huge handicap. Young people in Oakbank are very cliquey. They don't much care for people outside their tight social group. The partiers at this house party are prime examples of that. I'm an outsider and my presence is barely noticed. I'd take a nightclub over this frozen anonymity any day.

Further into the night, I find myself separated from Ratboy. I'm being a wallflower in the kitchen when I notice a bonfire in the backyard. I weave through the partiers and head outside. I find an empty lawn chair and sit by the fire. I light a cigarette, and when that one's done I light another, and another. I've been sitting there for almost an hour before the girl next to me turns and says, "Having fun?"

I turn and smile.

"Do I look like I'm having fun?" I ask.

"You look like you're having about as much fun as I am."

"You work at the hotel restaurant, right?"

"Yes. You work at the CountryGas station, right?"

"Unfortunately," I say. "So why are you here?"

The girl laughs.

"I live here," she says. "My parents thought they'd be

fun and throw me a surprise birthday party."

"Happy birthday."

"Thanks."

"How old are you?"

"Eighteen."

"Shit. I don't even remember my eighteenth birthday."

"Lucky you," she says. "All these people are here to celebrate me, and I just want them all to go away. I'd go crawl into my bed but there's probably people feeling each other up in it."

"What's your name?" I ask the girl.

"Carol," Carol says.

"Carol, you're the first genuine person I've ever met at one of these kinds of parties," I say.

She smiles.

"Really?"

"Yeah," I say. "Most girls on their eighteenth get really drunk and make really bad decisions. They don't sit by themselves and stare into a fire and contemplate their place in the world. You're awesome. You're going to be just fine."

There's silence for a while.

"Thanks," Carol says.

CHAPTER 06

A man in a suit walks into the store, walks up to the counter and stares at me.

"Yes?" I say.

"Cigarettes," he says.

I turn and look at the large display of cigarettes behind me. I turn back to the customer.

"What kind of cigarettes would you like?" I ask.

The man in the suit looks completely put out.

"I come in here every day and get the same cigarettes. Every day you ask me what kind. No wonder you're a fucking gas jockey. You'd never make it in the real world. Can't even remember one simple thing," he says.

"Sorry, what brand was that?" I ask.

The man looks like he's going to have a stroke and die. I'm kind of hoping he does. After a minute, he calms himself.

"DuMaurier. King size," he says.

I give him his smokes and take his money. I give him his change, and he leaves.

Shane is laughing at me.

"Why don't you just give him his smokes when he comes in?" he asks.

"'Cause fuck him, that's why," I say. "He's not special. This is a store. People come in, they tell us what they want and then we give it to them. Why should he get preferential treatment? I'm not his slave."

"I think you just like fucking with the customers," Shane says.

"You're not wrong there," I say.

I'd like to be proud of what I do. It's hard, though, when you look around and see what we sell. Gas, which contributes to the greenhouse emissions that are killing the planet. Cigarettes, which cause cancer and heart disease. Junk food and pop, which lead to obesity, diabetes, heart disease and cancer. Lotto tickets, which lead to the false hope that your fat, polluting, cancerous ass is going to be a millionaire. We don't sell a single thing to be proud of. We sell poison.

After work, I sleep. After sleeping, I write. At

dinnertime, I make dinner. I make fettuccini alfredo with chicken. My dad seems less displeased with his meal than he usually is.

"So, when are you going to come work with me?" he asks as we eat. "My boss is always looking for new labourers."

"No thanks, Dad," I say.

"What, are you going to work at the fucking gas station forever, leaching off me forever?" he says.

"Who's leaching off you? I have plenty of money," I say.

This is true. I have thousands of dollars in the bank. When you work five days a week at a job you walk to and you use your truck only once in a while, combined with next to no bills, then yeah, you save some pretty serious cash.

"Maybe you can buy groceries once in a while, then," my dad says.

"And maybe you can fucking cook for once," I say.

My dad slams his fist on the table. I don't flinch.

"Don't swear at me, boy," he says. "I just want you to think about your future."

"I think about my future all the time, Dad," I say.

"But you don't do nothing about it," he says. "You work at the fucking gas station, and then you come here and sleep. Thinking and acting are two different things."

"I'm taking a university class, Dad. You ever been to university?" I ask.

"I was too busy working with my hands, like a real man, to go to university," he says. "What're you taking at the university?"

"I'm taking a writing class," I say.

My dad smiles.

"Well, that'll come in real handy when the writing factories start hiring," he says.

CHAPTER 07

"You're up," Shane says.

I look at the clock. It's my hour to pump gas. Shane and I alternate hours. I fold up the newspaper I was reading and head outside. When I approach the car at pump one, the female driver is already out and walking toward the store.

"Twenty dollars, please," she says.

"Sure thing," I say.

I start pumping her gas. I'm only at ten bucks when she comes out of the store after having paid for her gas and walks past me.

"Thanks," she says.

She gets into her car and starts the engine. I'm still

fucking pumping. I click off the nozzle and pull it from her car. And not a second too soon, too, 'cause she drives off, leaving me standing with the nozzle and her gas cap, utterly buttfuckingly bewildered.

I look at the pump. I got to $14.34. I hang up the nozzle and go inside.

"What happened there?" Shane asks.

"Don't ask," I say.

Today is Wednesday. After work, after my nap and after I make dinner, I head into the city for class. Anne doesn't show up. I'm disappointed. I wonder if she'll ever come back. She seems the type that would just disappear forever.

When it's my time to share, I read the story that I've been working on this past week, a story about a young man who has a heart-to-heart chat with the elderly man who lives across the hall from him in his apartment building. The young man and his girlfriend used to make the elderly man dinner together, but now the girlfriend is gone and the two men discuss love and loss. Everyone seems to enjoy the story. When I go home I feel pretty good about myself.

CHAPTER 08

It's Friday evening and I'm back at Jonas's getting drunk in preparation for getting drunk at the Oak later. I'm drinking a beer and playing some wrestling game against George on PlayStation. Marc and Davis come into the living room.

"Do you guys want to get some weed for later tonight?" Davis asks.

George and I look up from our game.

"You want money for weed?" George asks.

"No," Marc says. "Well, yeah. We'll all chip in. I know a guy. But only if you guys are cool with that. Are you guys cool with that?"

George and I look at each other.

"Where's this coming from?" I ask.

"We were talking this week about what was more rock 'n' roll, booze or drugs. We figured drugs were more rock 'n' roll. You can't be a rock star if you don't do drugs at least sometimes," Davis says.

"Know what's really rock 'n roll?" I ask.

Marc and Davis look at me with blank expressions.

"Playing rock 'n roll music," I say.

"Yeah, that and doing drugs," Marc says.

"How much do you need?" George asks.

"Ten bucks each."

He groans and pulls a ten out of his wallet.

Marc turns to me.

"You in?" he asks.

I cough up ten dollars.

I've never had much of an appetite for drugs. In high school I smoked pot and oil from time to time, but I've always preferred to mess myself up with beer. I like how I feel when I'm drunk off beer. It's predictable. I know how I'm going to act when I'm drunk. Drugs can go sideways on you pretty quick.

I try to remember the last time I smoked pot. Oh right. It was the night I felt up Amy. Great. Now I'm depressed again.

Marc and Davis take their money and disappear for half an hour and return with a bag of weed. We leave it at

Jonas's and head to the bar. I drink beers and count the minutes till it's time to leave.

At the end of the night, the five of us regroup in the parking lot and start the thirty-minute walk back to Jonas's. Once there, Marc rolls up a joint on the kitchen table and passes it around. When the joint is pretty much cashed, I start to feel funny. My mouth dries right the fuck out and my head starts spinning. I slowly rise from the table.

"You okay, buddy?" George asks.

"Gonna go puke," I say.

And I do. That night I sleep on Jonas's bathroom floor.

CHAPTER 09

"What happened last night?" George asks.

We're sitting at a table in Perkins. George has eggs and bacon and sausage and hash browns and toast on a plate in front of him. I have coffee.

"I don't know, man," I say. "I felt like shit as soon as we smoked that joint. I didn't even drink that much."

"Sometimes mixing makes people sick," he says.

"It never bothered me in high school," I say.

"People change."

"Maybe I'm getting old."

"You don't look a day over thirty."

"Thanks."

George drops me off at home after breakfast. I go to

my room and sleep until my dad bangs on my door and tells me I have a phone call. I get up and stagger down to the phone in the kitchen. I'm pleased to hear my friend Fiona's voice at the other end.

"How's it going, Brendan?" she asks.

"I'm okay. You?"

"I'm good. My plans for tonight kinda fell through. You wanna get together for coffee or something?" she asks.

"Sure. Where?"

"Meet you at the hotel for seven?"

"Sounds good."

When I'm off the phone with Fiona, I look at the digital clock on the microwave. It's six o'clock now.

"Shit," I say and head to the bathroom for a shower.

Once I'm showered and clean and dressed, I walk to the hotel, smoking cigarettes. I arrive at the hotel restaurant to find Fiona already seated. I join her.

"How's it going, dude?" she asks, smiling.

"Still okay," I say. "What's new with you?"

"Not much," she says. "I normally hang out with Todd on Saturdays, but he has some kind of guys' night tonight so I thought I'd have a girls' night with you."

I make a face.

"Awesome," I say.

I've known Fiona forever. We went to school together,

from elementary to graduation. We didn't actually become tight, though, till after grad. I can't remember how it happened, but we just started hanging out together all the time. We'd go to the bar together, we'd go for coffee together, she'd even sleep over at my place. It was purely platonic. We'd stay up late and watch shitty TV shows. Then she got a boyfriend, a boyfriend who didn't see that I was no more a threat to him than Fiona's girlfriends. I saw a lot less of her. That's when I started hanging out more with George and the other Lost Astronaut guys.

Carol approaches our table, notepad in hand.

"Hey, Brendan," she says. "What can I get you?"

I haven't eaten since I threw up last night so I order a bacon cheeseburger and fries and an iced tea.

Carol turns to Fiona and asks, "And for you?"

"Just a coffee. Thanks," she says.

Carol smiles at me and leaves.

"So what's new with you, Brendan?" Fiona asks.

"Nothing."

"Nothing?"

"Not a thing."

"How is that possible?"

"It just is."

"I haven't seen you in forever. There must be something new and exciting in your life," Fiona says.

"Nope."

"Still working at the CountryGas?"

"Yup."

"How's that going?"

"It's like a Mensa meeting, but the opposite of that."

"Okay. You ever think of going back to school?"

"Not really."

"You should. You're too smart to be spending all your time in a gas station."

Fiona doesn't intend for this to be hurtful, but you know what they say about good intentions.

"I'm actually taking a university course now," I say.

Fiona's face lights up.

"What are you taking?" she asks.

"It's a creative writing class through Continuing Education at the U of W. We meet every Wednesday night," I say.

"Cool. You like it?"

"Yeah. I do."

"Any cute girls?"

"Everyone's older. There's one girl who's —"

"What?"

"— interesting."

"Well, that sounds interesting," Fiona says.

Carol arrives with a coffee and an iced tea. We thank her and she leaves.

"So, what's so interesting about this girl?" Fiona asks.

"I don't know," I say. "She's not like most people. She talks really monotone and it's hard to tell whether she's being sarcastic or not. She seems really smart and worldly like she's actually seen shit and done shit."

"Is she pretty?"

"She's really pretty."

"What's really pretty about her?"

"The fact that she doesn't care whether people think she's pretty or not," I say.

"She seems nice," Fiona says.

That's the last we talk about Anne. Fiona fills me in on what's going on with her, with school and with Todd, and before long my food arrives. When the bill arrives, I take care of it.

Fiona and I are standing at the door, about to leave, when Carol comes up to me.

"Thanks for being cool the other night," she says. Then she plants a little kiss on my cheek.

"No problem, lady," I say.

Carol smiles and heads back to work.

Fiona looks impressed.

"What was all that about?" she asks.

"Don't worry about it."

CHAPTER 10

It's been two weeks since 9/11. That's what we call the terrorist attacks now. 9/11. The news tells me that a guy named Osama bin Laden is to blame, him and his al-Qaeda terrorist network. The news tells me he's hiding out in Afghanistan and there's a very high likelihood that we may be sending troops there.

Basically, shit is hitting the fan on a global scale.

It's Tuesday morning and I'm outside the gas station, staring at nothing. An oldtimer walks past me and says, "We live in a very different world now."

I nod at him. "You said it."

CHAPTER 11

It's the end of class. Kate stands and says, "Next week, bring in the piece you are most proud of, everyone, and we'll really deconstruct it and build it up and make it the best piece of writing it can be."

I grab my notebook and head for the door. Anne follows me into the hall.

"You wanna go for coffee again, Brendan?" she asks.

"You wanna go for coffee with me?" I ask.

"Yeah."

"Where were you last week?"

"I wasn't feeling well."

"That sucks."

We're outside now. I light a cigarette. Anne lights one of her own.

"Why do you wanna have coffee with me, Anne?" I ask.

"'Cause I like having coffee with you," she says.

I weigh this in my brain a little while.

"Fair enough," I say.

So we walk to the little café we went to two weeks ago and sit at the same table we sat at last time. Anne orders a black coffee, and I order a coffee and a slice of banana cream pie.

"So, what were you sick with?" I ask her.

"I was sick with the world," she says.

"Yeah. I get that sometimes," I say.

Our coffees arrive. Anne drinks hers without letting it cool.

"What do you like most about writing?" she asks me.

"I don't know," I say. "I just like it."

Anne is staring at me. She doesn't blink. It's unnerving.

"Would you like me to leave?" she asks.

"Why would I want you to leave?"

"I could have more stimulating conversation with the walls of my apartment."

"I bet you have."

"What do you like most about writing?" she asks me again.

I close my eyes for a moment and reopen them.

"I wasn't the happiest kid in the world. My mom left when I was nine, and my dad is a complete dick. Writing was my escape. I could lose myself in it, in the characters and storylines. When I was writing, I wasn't the loser I was in real life. I was creating something. Y'know?" I say.

"Yeah," Anne says, lighting a cigarette. "I know."

I light one, too.

"How 'bout you? What do you like most about writing?" I ask.

"I like that it's the only thing in the world that I can do well," she says. "I like that it never lets me down."

I tap my lighter on the table for a little while.

"Anne," I say.

"Yeah?"

"There's something that's been eating at me for a while," I say. "I was wondering if maybe I could get your input on it."

"Okay."

"It's about this girl, Amy."

I tell Anne the Amy story. When I'm done, Anne looks unimpressed.

"So you touched a girl's boob and you feel bad about it?" she says.

"It was uninvited. That's like rape."

"Did you rape this girl?"

"Well, no."

"Did you throw her down in the bushes and stick your dick in her?"

"Jesus fuck, no."

"Then you didn't rape her," Anne says. "I'm not saying what you did wasn't wrong, but don't beat yourself up forever about it."

"What should I do, then?"

She smiles.

"You ever consider apologizing to this girl?"

"How do I do that? What should I say?"

"You're a smart guy. You'll figure it out."

CHAPTER 12

I'm washing the windshield of a giant truck. The owner of the truck is standing beside me, watching me. The gas is done and he's just waiting for me to finish up with the squeegee so he can leave.

"You're doing it wrong," he says.

"Yeah?" I say. I love when people criticize the work I've been doing for three fucking years.

"Yeah," the asshole customer says. "You're leaving some wetness at the bottom of the windshield by the wipers. This is how you do it properly."

He takes the squeegee from me and starts dragging it across his windshield horizontally from the centre, leaving a long wet mark vertically down his window.

"Do you not see what you're doing there?" I say, pointing at the mark.

"This is how you do it properly," he says.

He goes to hand the squeegee back to me, but I just walk away.

"You've got to take pride in your work, even if you're just pumping gas," the man says to my back.

It takes all of my restraint to keep from giving him the finger.

A few hours later, I'm almost done my shift when this kid walks up to the counter with a box of Pixie Sticks. He plops it down in front of me.

"How much are these?" he asks.

"They're ten cents each," I tell him.

"How much is the whole box?" he asks.

"You want the whole box?"

"Yeah."

I try to gauge the age of this kid. He's young enough to want Pixie Sticks but old enough to know better.

"You know this is just sugar and food colouring, right?" I say.

"So?"

"Do you know what diabetes is?"

"Not really."

"You will."

"Do you want to make this sale or not?" the kid asks me.

I ring in the box of Pixie Sticks.

"Hey, it's your funeral, man," I say.

I turn my attention to the next asshole customer in line. Son of a bitch, it's Marissa. Goddammit. That little kid distracted me.

"How's it going, Brendan?" she asks, approaching the counter.

"Not bad, Marissa," I say. "How are you?"

"I'm good," she says.

I bet you are, bitch.

"I haven't seen you here in a while. I thought maybe you got another job," she says.

"Nope. Still here," I say. "You getting gas?"

"Yeah."

I look to the machine under the window. Still filling. Fuck.

"Crazy about what's going on in the States, huh?" Marissa says.

Are you fucking serious?

"Yeah, really crazy," I say.

"Do you still hang out with Davis?" she asks.

Why, do you want to fuck him, too?

"On the weekends, yeah," I say.

"That's good," she says.

The machine beeps to let me know her gas is done, and I ring her through and say goodbye.

"Take care of yourself, Brendan," she says as she leaves.

Fuck you.

Shane comes back in.

"Sorry, man," he says. "I tried to warn you."

"It's cool," I say.

"Why doesn't she go to a different gas station?" he asks.

"I have no fucking clue, man," I say.

"You wanna come to the bar tonight?" he asks. "A few of us are going."

Suddenly I really feel like having a beer.

"Yeah. Okay."

"Awesome."

Our replacements come in just before noon, and then I walk home, smoking cigarettes as I go. Not to break tradition, when I get home, I sleep for a while, and then I get up, shower and make dinner. My dad and I eat together at the kitchen table in silence. When he's done, he grabs a beer from the fridge and retires to his chair in the living room. I do the dishes, then put on my jacket.

"Where you going?" my dad asks, never taking his eyes off the TV.

"I'm meeting some people from work at the bar," I say.

"Don't piss all your money away," he says.

I laugh.

"Do you not see the irony in that? You saying that while sitting on your ass drinking a beer?" I say.

"I earn my beers by working hard every day," my dad says. "Can you say that?"

"Bye, Dad," I say, and I leave.

Two cigarettes' worth of walking later, I'm at the bar in the hotel. Shane, Erica and a couple of others we work with, Matty and Chantelle, are already seated. I join them.

Davis, Kyle and I started coming to the hotel bar when we were sixteen. The owners then didn't much care if you were underage so long as you spent money. They used to have one-dollar shots on Saturday nights. We called it buckshot. You could get a rum and coke for a dollar, or a double for two, etc. You could get right shit-tanked for less than twenty bucks. It was great. Those were the days.

Liquor laws have changed since then, and so have the owners of the bar, and while it takes a little more money to get shit-tanked now, at least the new owners have put that extra drink money into renovating the bar. It's not so much of a dive now.

I'm sitting next to Erica.

"How's it going, Brendan?" she asks.

"I'm okay. You?"

"Not bad."

Erica feels awkward around me. Because of the whole telling me about Marissa thing. I remember her first words to me about it were, "Please don't hate me, but ..." I don't hate Erica. I'm grateful to her. Had she not told me what was going on, I might still be with Marissa, oblivious to the fact that she was fucking other guys. And I could have gonorrhea. Nobody wants gonorrhea.

"What are you drinking, Erica?" I ask.

"Vodka sev," she says.

"Cool," I say. I go up to the bar, and I get a beer and a vodka 7-Up. I give Erica her drink.

"What's this for?" she asks.

"For being great."

"Thanks, Brendan."

"No problem."

I like these guys. They've all known each other forever, from going to school together in Oakbank, and they make me feel like one of them. There's no weirdness from them, not like with others from my "hometown." They don't treat me like an outsider. With them, I'm just one of the gang. Aside from Erica's awkwardness, everything is cool.

We sit and drink most of the night. Around midnight, Shane and I leave. We've got to open the store in the morning.

CHAPTER 13

For class on Wednesday, I bring the first chapter of my novel to be critiqued. I'm so excited that I volunteer to read first. The chapter goes like so:

I was immortalized on televisions across the country. I was the symbol of what was a great tragedy, like the guy who stood before the tanks at Tiananmen Square or the Vietnamese girl who ran naked from her napalmed village. I was an image burned into the consciousness of a nation as seen on TV during the evening news. I became a sort of hero to many, and I didn't know it. At the time, I didn't know whether I was alive or dead, whether the images I registered before all faded to black were apparitions or real, able to be touched, tasted or felt under more suitable circumstances.

Though I was rapidly losing consciousness, I was well aware of the pain that wracked my body. White-hot fire seared through my guts, the sensation radiating over my torso in waves as if my body were dry, dead wood. My head and knee throbbed unbearably, blood from high above my hairline flowing down my face, joining the gore that poured from my nose. The crimson liquid collected and hit the pavement in a steady stream, stretching out before my half-open, tear-filled eyes. I was only half there mentally, but I remember the blood looked almost black as it formed a pool next to my face, deeper and darker than any ocean on the planet.

I was also aware of that which I couldn't feel as I lay there that afternoon. My arm, twisted unnaturally beneath my body, was eerily numb. Any effort to move it was fruitless. Any attempt to roll off of it was met by electric shocks of agony coursing through nerves to my every extremity — save, of course, the arm.

And then very abruptly, as if I were suddenly plunged into freezing water, the numbness consumed my entire body at once, extinguishing the flames at the pit of me, easing the throbbing to a dull pain in my head and knee. The abyss of black blood continued to grow before me until it swallowed my entire ever-blurring field of vision, until all that was left to be seen before sight was lost to me was darkness.

Then nothing.

High above where my body lay broken and bloody, the news camera rolled, and I didn't know. I lay unconscious, dead to the world, and the camera recorded every second. The paramedics couldn't reach me, nor could the police, not at the time, but the intrusive unblinking eye could. It hungered, sopping up all it could, the blood, the fear, the chaos that unfolded below. That fateful afternoon, the cameras fed.

I remember the date well because it had been drilled into my mind for months, since the beginning of the semester. April second, the day my term paper was due. Had I not fucked around so much, getting drunk and getting laid, then maybe I wouldn't have been hiding out in the library putting the sloppy finishing touches on a project that was really only three quarters complete and would probably net me fifty-five percent at the most.

I sat there, my mind reeling, one hand scribbling down words that were no more than chicken scratches on paper, the other hand flipping through encyclopedias, history books and nonsense notes at an inhuman pace. My eyes darted from one page to the next, sore and bloodshot and fighting to stay open. I was so engrossed that I didn't notice when Tyler Brooks arrived at my table all wide eyed and *puffing from physical exertion.*

Or fear.

He slammed his palms down on my table more to stop his momentum than to gain my attention. At the time, not knowing the severity of the situation, I found it annoying. I didn't like Tyler Brooks, and I knew it was him without even looking up. I'd like to think I didn't like him because his track pants were several sizes too big and would brush up against me when passing in the hall. Or maybe because the extensions in his hair looked like frayed rope, or because he made everyone call him T-Bone. I'd like to think I didn't like him because he was a rich kid from the south end of the city, but he talked, acted and dressed like a homeboy straight off the streets of Compton. I'd like to think it was all of those reasons, but it wasn't.

I didn't like Tyler Brooks because he was a nigger.

There were a couple gasps in the room. I pause for a moment, then continue on.

The truth is I didn't solely dislike Tyler Brooks because he was black, but more because of the person he believed himself to be because of his race. As I scrambled to complete my paper, however, my hostility towards him had nothing to do with the colour of his skin. I would have been pissed off if Christ Himself had interrupted me.

Kate stands.

"How 'bout we stop right there," she says. "Class, what do you think of what Brendan just shared?"

The hippie to my right speaks first.

"I just don't like that word," she says.

"Which word?" the man in the wheelchair says.

"The N word," she says.

There're murmurs of agreement throughout the room.

"Couldn't you use a nicer word? Something better?" the hippie asks.

"I suppose I could," I say.

"Don't listen to her, Brendan," the wheelchair man says. "Don't censor yourself. Use whatever words you want."

"I just think he'd be doing himself a disservice," the hippie says. "People don't like writers who use that word."

"So people don't like Mark Twain, or John Steinbeck, or Harper Lee?" the wheelchair man says.

"That's different," the hippie says. "What he wrote is racist."

"Yeah, it is," I say. "It's supposed to be. The main character is racist."

The hippie turns to me.

"Why would you make your main character racist?" she asks.

"I don't know," I say. "I really like the movie *Taxi Driver*, and Robert DeNiro's character in *Taxi Driver* is racist. I thought that's a really great flaw for a main character to have. A really shitty thing happens to the main character in my book, and you want to feel bad for him but he's such a piece of shit that the reader becomes conflicted. I didn't want to write a black-and-white book. So to speak."

I look across the room. Anne is smiling at me. I look to Kate, and she's smiling, too.

"Why don't you finish your piece, Brendan," she says.

And I do.

At the end of the class, Anne comes up to me.

"You wanna hang out, or do you have a KKK meeting to go to?" she asks.

"Funny," I say. "No. I'm free."

"Cool. Wanna come to my place and watch a movie?" she asks.

"Sure."

"Did you drive here? 'Cause I took the bus."

"Yeah, I've got my truck here."

"Good. Let's go, then."

The whole way to Anne's apartment, I'm trying to figure out what *watch a movie* means. I know what it means for guys. It means, *Would you like to come to my place and have sex?* I'm not sure what it means to Anne. She's definitely not a guy and she's not like most girls I know, so it could mean anything. Or it could mean that we're going to watch a movie. I decide to play it cool and take things at face value.

We park at an apartment near Corydon. We go inside. Anne's suite is spacious and furnished, and the decorating is very basic. There's an entertainment unit with a TV and a stereo. There's a couch and a chair beside it. There's a rug over the hardwood with a coffee table on it. There's a bookshelf against a wall, and I walk over to it. There're a lot of books by Noam Chomsky and Howard Zinn. There're a lot of books with anarchism in the title. That makes sense.

I turn to see Anne holding up a DVD copy of the film *Memento*.

"Have you seen this?" she asks.

"Yeah. It's great," I say.

"You wanna watch it again?"

"Sure."

Anne motions to the couch and tells me to sit, and I do. She puts the movie in her DVD player and comes back and sits on the chair beside me.

We watch the movie. That's all that happens. When it's over I turn and see that Anne has fallen asleep. I shake her arm and tell her I'm leaving. She murmurs something unintelligible, turns over and curls up in the fetal position on the chair.

"You're weird," I tell her. Then I leave.

CHAPTER 14

Anne doesn't show up to class the next Wednesday. I sit and listen to people read their pieces and I wonder about this absence, and then I go home to sleep. That weekend, I hang out with my friends while they drink and talk to girls and smoke pot in varying locations. The next week begins and I pump gas and drink coffee and bottles of water while I read the papers. When Wednesday gets its turn on the calendar, I spend most of the morning at work wondering whether Anne will be at class tonight.

I overfill four cars. I almost never do that.

CHAPTER 15

Two minutes before the class is set to start, Anne rushes in and sits in her spot across from me. She doesn't look up from her notebook. When it's her turn to share, she reads a piece called "Endless Sleep" that I glean is about death. At break time she gets up and heads out the door, presumably to go out on the sidewalk and smoke. I stay in my seat. She doesn't come back from break.

After class, I'm out the door and walking to my truck. I notice someone's walking behind me.

"You didn't come outside at break," Anne says.

"No, I didn't," I say.

"Why not?"

"Why weren't you in class last week?"

"I didn't know I had to be."

"You're paying for this class. If you want to get anything from it, you have to show up."

"Thanks, Dad."

I stop walking and turn to face Anne. She nearly walks into me.

"This is really frustrating, Anne," I say.

She's glaring at me. She steps even closer to me than she already is. We're the same height. So are our crotches. I look away.

"How frustrating is it? Do you want to fuck me? Is that it?" she says.

I turn around and keep walking.

"That's not it at all," I say.

"Then what is it?"

"You're smart. You'll figure it out."

I'm at my truck, unlocking my door. Anne's still standing back where we stopped.

"Brendan ..."

"What?"

"I'm sorry."

"For what?"

"For being a lady dick."

"That's fine. You're forgiven. Goodnight."

"Can we talk?"

I've got my driver's side door open. I'm about to get in and be done with it.

Instead I say, "Okay."

We go to our café and grab our table. The waitress brings us coffees.

"What's up?" I ask.

"I have insomnia, Brendan," Anne says.

"But you're awake," I say.

She glares at me. I shake my head.

"Sorry, that was stupid," I say. "How long have you had insomnia?"

"For about a year," she says. "I feel tired, but when I go to bed, I just lie there. I sleep very little when I do, but usually I don't sleep at all. Either I lie there or I get up and read or clean or anything. I'm wired all the time. My eyes feel like they're bugging out of my skull. I see movement out of the corner of my eye when I'm alone, and I turn and nothing's there. I've lost twenty pounds. I used to be curvy. Now I look like a Holocaust victim."

"I think you look great," I say.

The glare returns.

"Gee. Thanks," Anne says.

"You slept the other night when we watched *Memento*," I say.

She lights a cigarette.

"That's what I'm getting to," she says. "I slept

amazingly that night. I slept a full eight hours. I dreamt. Do you know how long it's been since I had a dream? I woke up feeling rested. I felt amazing. I didn't even care I was two hours late for work."

"What do you do, by the way?"

"Who cares?" Anne says. "The important thing is that I slept like a normal human being and it was great. I thought I was cured. I was excited to go to bed the next night, but nothing happened. I tossed and turned the entire night. And the night after that. And after that. I haven't slept more than ten hours in the last two weeks."

"Shitty," I say. "So what was special about the night you slept?"

Anne is smiling at me. She points at me with her cigarette.

"Me?" I say.

"Yes."

"What did I do?"

"I have no idea. But you're the only variable that makes sense."

"That doesn't make sense."

"No? I've done everything and anything to fall asleep. I've tried pills, therapy, movies, music, pot, oil, wine, masturbation, everything, and nothing has worked. Then you sit with me and I'm out like a light," Anne says.

"Did you try giving up black coffee and cigarettes?"

"I did. I tried *everything*," she says.

"I see where this is going," I say, lighting a cigarette. "You want to kill me, stuff me and strap me to your couch."

She nods.

"That's an option," she says. "For now, though, how 'bout you just come over tonight. Of your own volition."

"You wanna have a slumber party?"

"I do. So much. You'd really be helping me out."

So that's what we do. We sleep together. Literally. Anne falls asleep first. When she's out, I reach over and set her alarm clock (which she probably hasn't used in a year) to five o'clock. Then I'm asleep, too. When the alarm goes off in the morning, my hand darts out and shuts it off. I roll over and look at Anne. She's still asleep in her clothes. I reset the alarm to seven o'clock. Then I'm up and gone.

CHAPTER 16

It's Friday night and I'm sitting on a high stool at a high round table in an elevated part of the Oak, beside the DJ booth. I'm sitting alone, drinking a beer, smoking. From my high vantage point, I can see Amy sitting at a table with three other women. I leave my beer bottle on the table and I take my cigarette with me over to Amy's table.

I lean in to talk to her over the music.

"Wanna go outside and talk?" I shout into her ear.

She looks at me, nods, gets up and heads for the exit. I follow.

Outside, she's sitting on the curb. I sit next to her.

"I think I know what this is about," she says.

"Yeah," I say.

"You're in love with me," she says.

"Wait. What?" I say.

"Are you in love with me?"

"Um, no. I think you're great, but that's not why I brought you out here," I say.

"Oh."

"I want to talk about Birds Hill Park."

"Ohhhhhhhhh."

"I grabbed you and it was wrong and I feel really bad about it. I'm sorry I did that to you and I'd like to make it up to you any way that I can," I say.

Amy's silent a moment. Then she starts to cry.

"I've been taken advantage of by a lot by guys," she says. "I never thought you'd be one of those guys, Brendan."

There's a hard, jagged lump in my throat.

"I'm sorry," I say again.

"You weren't sorry the next day," she says.

"Huh?"

"Travis Gordry said you were bragging about feeling me up the next day at breakfast," she says.

My mind is making that crazy sound VHS players make when you're rewinding at high speed. Stop. Play.

"I remember that," I say. "I was talking to Travis about it because I felt bad and wanted to talk about it, and Kyle was there and he was like, 'Does she have nice tits?' and to make him go away I was like, 'Yeah, Kyle, she has nice tits.'"

Her face wet with tears, Amy turns to me, smiling.

"You think I have nice tits?" she asks.

"Um. Sure."

She hugs me and leaves one arm around me when she pulls away.

"You were really drunk that night. I was really drunk. Everyone was. Bad decisions were made, but you're not a bad guy, so I forgive you, Brendan," she says.

"Thank you."

Amy stands.

"You wanna go do a shot?" she asks.

I light a new cigarette, then shake my head.

"I'm just going to sit here a little while," I say.

Amy wipes the tears from her face and smiles.

"Okay. See you inside," she says, and then she's inside.

Smoking alone on the curb, I mutter, "What the fuck?"

CHAPTER 17

I'm at the gas station. I'm outside, pouring a litre of oil down a funnel into the engine of a van. The owner of the van is standing beside me, watching. When the oil bottle is empty, I throw it into the garbage that stands between the two pumps. When I pull the funnel away from the man's van, a drop of oil lands on the bumper.

"What the hell is that?" the man demands, pointing directly at the small glob of brown on his bumper. His fingertip is an inch away.

"Sorry," I say.

"You're going to be sorry," he says.

This has nothing to do with the tiny spot of engine oil. This has nothing to do with me. Not really. This has everything to do with the man. He's wearing a suit. It's a decent suit but not really nice, so I glean that this man has an important job but not really important. He probably has more people above him giving him shit than he has below him to give shit, so shit like what's happening now happens far too often with him. He'll go to a movie, say, and lose it when they spill his popcorn. He'll go to a restaurant and ask to see the manager when the waitress brings him a Budweiser instead of a Bud Lite. He spends a lot of time on the phone yelling at people he'll never have to face in real life. This is how he gets through the day. He's a total fucking prick.

I walk over to the paper towel dispenser and grab a paper towel. I walk back to the van.

"You bet your fucking ass you're going to clean that up," the man says. "That shit'll eat right through the paint."

I wipe off the oil. Then I stand up straight and move close to the man. I'm five foot ten and two hundred pounds of mostly bone and muscle. I don't like to have to intimidate people, but fuck this guy.

"Maybe you'd feel more comfortable getting gas at a different gas station," I say quietly.

I see a brief flash of terror in the man's eyes and I smile. Fast as a human being can move, he's at his driver's side door.

"Don't worry. I will," he says as he gets into his van.

"You take care," I say.

And he's gone.

CHAPTER 18

"You're in my seat," Anne says to the hippie to my right.

The hippie looks up at her, confused.

"But I always sit here," she says.

"It's called change. Roll with it," Anne says. "We're switching spots."

The hippie grumbles and gathers some papers and goes and sits across from me where Anne used to sit. Anne slumps down next to me. I look over at the wheelchair man. He smiles, then looks away, still smiling.

We're ten minutes into class when Anne slides a note over.

Coming over tonight?

I give her a thumbs up.

And so, in accordance with the note and with my thumbs up, after class I drive Anne and myself to Anne's apartment off Corydon. Once home, Anne kicks off her shoes and throws her coat on the hardwood floor. I'm in Rome, so I do as Anne does. I join her in the living room.

"You wanna go to bed right away or watch a movie first or what?" I ask.

Anne makes a face and walks over to her entertainment unit.

"I don't really feel like going to bed yet," she says, powering on her stereo. "What kind of music do you like?"

"I like Elliott Smith," I say.

"Just Elliott Smith?"

"Yeah."

"The *Good Will Hunting* guy?"

Now I make a face.

"Yeah, he has some songs on the soundtrack, but he's more than just the *Good Will Hunting* guy. He was in a band called Heatmiser and he's really done well for himself as a solo artist. That's how Gus Van Sant heard of him and …"

Anne cuts me off.

"Don't be a pretentious douche," she says. "You heard of him because of *Good Will Hunting*. If not for that movie, you wouldn't know who the fuck Elliott Smith is."

I lower my head.

"You are not incorrect," I say.

"Well, I don't have any Elliott Smith, or any Heatmiser for that matter," she says. "What else do you listen to?"

"That's pretty much all I listen to."

"That's weird."

"Thanks. I used to listen to punk," I say feebly.

Anne's eyebrows rise and she turns back to her stereo.

"Oooooo. Punk, I have," she says.

After some shuffling of CD cases and some opening and closing of her CD player's disc tray, raunchy, fast guitars come through Anne's speakers. She tells me to sit on the couch, and when I do, she sits next to me.

"Who is this?" I ask.

"The Distillers," Anne says.

The singing starts, and while rough, the voice is distinctly female. The first song, I gather, is about a strong woman named Serena, and I understand why Anne likes the band. They charge along at a wonderfully fast pace and the songs' choruses beg to be sung with a fist raised high.

When the CD ends, Anne puts on another.

"You might like this, too," she says, sitting again.

The room fills with dark, ominous guitars and driving drums. Anne tells me the band is called Alkaline Trio. The album is *From Here to Infirmary*. The song we're listening to is "Private Eye." By the chorus, I'm in love.

With the band, that is.

We chat while the CD plays, and when it ends, Anne puts on a disc called *A Flight and a Crash* by a band called Hot Water Music. The first song hooks me immediately.

Anne sits again.

"I thought punk rock now was all Blink 182 and Good Charlotte bullshit," I say. "I didn't know there are still good bands out there."

"There are. You just have to dig a little deeper for them," she says.

We're quiet for a little while, listening.

"I spoke to that Amy girl," I say. "I apologized to her."

"Good for you," Anne says. "How'd that go?"

"Really weird and awkward, actually."

"How so?"

"She thought I was going to profess my love for her. Then when I brought up the incident, she started crying. Then for some reason I told her she has nice boobs, and she seemed to enjoy that I said that. Then she forgave me and asked if I wanted to do a shot with her. Kinda fucked, right?" I say.

Anne is silent a moment. Then she says, "Gloria Steinem once said, 'One woman's date rape sometimes is another woman's bad night.'"

"Gloria Steinem said that?"

"I think so. Or maybe it was someone else. Point is, as you get older, you find that not everything is black and white. In the real world, there's a fuckload of grey. What you did wasn't the best thing that ever happened, but you felt bad and you made amends, and I think that shows a lot about your character. Tonight, a bunch of fucking bros are going to go to the bar and bro it up and get drunk and take home drunk girls and fuck them under questionable circumstances. And tomorrow they'll do the same thing, and the night after that and the night after that, and they won't think twice about it. Because, for whatever reason, they don't think that what they're doing is wrong. But I know it's wrong, and you know it's wrong, and people like us know it's wrong, and that's half the battle," Anne says.

She stands and changes the CD to a band she tells me is called Rise Against.

"I want to go to bed now," she tells me.

"You're going to leave the stereo on?" I ask.

"Yeah. Fuck it."

Anne falls asleep quickly beside me in her bed. I set her alarm clock to wake me up at five, then turn off her lamp. I settle back down in the bed. I turn and plant a kiss on Anne's temple.

"Goodnight," I say. Then I'm drifting off too.

CHAPTER 19

"You going on Saturday?" Shane asks me.

I'm sitting uncomfortably on the top step of the little three-step ladder we keep behind the counter at work. I'm drinking coffee. I'm very, very tired.

"Going where?"

"Halloween social. Saturday night," Shane says. "I've mentioned it at least five times already this morning,"

"Sorry," I say. "I'm very, very tired."

"Hungover?"

"No, just a late night."

"You want a ticket to the social or not?"

"Whose social?"

"Matty's friends Bev and Devin."

"Bev and Devin? That's their names? That's too perfect. They getting married?"

"Yeah."

"How old are they?"

"Twenty-four, I think."

"Christ. What's the rush?"

Shane laughs.

"Twenty-four is a very normal age to get married. It wasn't very long ago that people got married much younger. Just because you're stunted, doesn't mean others are too," he says.

I smile.

"I'm stunted?"

"Yes."

"Dude, we work the same job. We both live at home. We have basically the same social life. And you're four years older than me. C'mon. Who's really stunted here?" I ask.

"I mean you're emotionally stunted," Shane says.

"Oh," I say. "You're not wrong there."

Jane comes out of the back office. She sees me sitting on the stepladder and says nothing about it. One time, when I was working at the hardware store, I was putting price stickers on some of the merchandise. There was a stack of those circular plastic things that people take down ski hills. You know what I'm talking about. Anyway, there was a stack of them on the floor so I sat on the floor to put price stickers on them. My boss saw this and went ballistic, like she had walked over and witnessed me dismembering a customer on the linoleum.

"How will you ever get a job at Walmart or Canadian Tire if all you do is sit around?" she asked me.

Wow. Walmart? Canadian Tire? Be still, my heart.

Lesson learned: If your boss expects you to stand for eight hours straight during a shift, tell them to go fuck themselves with something long and sharp.

So yeah, Jane sees me sitting and it doesn't faze her because, as I've already stated, Jane is a sweetheart. She does inform us, though, that gas has gone up two cents, and she asks me to go out and change the sign.

Changing the sign involves a large plastic square with a number on it and a long pole with a suction cup on it. I apply the suction cup to the number already on the sign that needs changing out. I bring it down to ground level. Then I put the new number on the suction cup and raise it up to the sign. I slide the new number onto the track, pop off the suction cup and boom, sign is changed.

I turn to see that a middle-aged man is standing next to me, looking up at the sign.

"Gas going up, eh?" he says.

"Yep," I say.

"How do you know when to change it?" he asks.

"My boss tells me," I say.

"And who tells her?"

"She gets a call from Saudi Arabia."

The middle-aged man turns to me, wide eyed.

"Really?" he asks.

I shake my head.

"No," I say.

The man looks at me for an uncomfortable period of time. Then he swats me on the arm and laughs.

"Sure. Sure, buddy," he says. Then he makes his way next door to Agnew's Restaurant.

Fucking idiot.

Later in the morning, towards the end of the shift, I'm manning the counter while Shane is out pumping gas. A guy about ten years older than me plops a newspaper in front of me. Osama bin Laden is on the cover.

I look up at the asshole customer. He's looking very intently at me.

"Eighty cents," I tell him.

He hands me a loonie.

"Crazy what's going on in the Middle East, eh?" the customer says.

I nod.

"You're Middle Eastern, aren't you?" he says.

I smile. I get this a lot. My mom is Italian, so I'm not quite as white as the average white-bread assholes that make up Oakbank's population. People will try to guess my ethnicity, as if I'll be really amazed and impressed if they get it right. I've gotten Israeli, Palestinian, Brazilian, Puerto Rican, Indian, Portuguese, fucking everything ... everything except, of course, half Italian. People always seem really disappointed when I tell them the truth.

"I'm actually half Italian," I tell the asshole customer.

He scoops up his paper and smiles.

"Isn't that what Middle Eastern people say when they don't want people to know they're Middle Eastern?" he says. "Don't worry, pal. Your secret's safe with me."

The asshole gives me the wink and the gun, and he's out the door.

Alone, I mutter to myself, "I'm going to get fucking shot, aren't I?"

CHAPTER 20

After work on Friday, before George comes to pick me up, I watch the news. The news now plays out like the fake news in some shitty action movie. Terrorist attacks, anthrax attacks, invading Afghanistan, citizens stocking up on rations and gas masks: this is all Hollywood shit. Except it's not. This is the new reality. I have to check several times to make sure that the CNN logo is at the bottom of the screen, that I'm not watching a Tony Scott movie.

I watch a speech by George W. Bush. When he was first elected, all you saw on *Saturday Night Live* or *The Daily Show* was skits and segments on how much of a fucking idiot he is. Now he's leading troops from allied nations (including Canada) against the threat of terrorism.

I have a feeling this is going to end badly for everyone involved.

CHAPTER 21

I did end up buying a social ticket from Shane, so Saturday evening I'm driving my shitty B2000 truck south on Highway 206 to Dugald. Dugald is the next town over from Oakbank. It's where I went to elementary school. In fact, the community club I'm heading to is directly across the street from my old school. I used to go to the community club for dances when I was a kid. I'd dance an arm's length apart from girls in my grade while a DJ played Guns N Roses and Mr. Big. Those dances were the most fun I would have until I discovered underage drinking, smoking and drugs. Good times.

In case you've never been to the vast metropolis of Winnipeg (and why wouldn't you?), or anywhere in

Manitoba for that matter, you may not know what a social is. Socials exist so that when a couple is getting married, they can raise some money to offset the cost of their wedding. The couple rents a hall a few months before their big day, they buy a bunch of booze and silent auction prizes, and then they sell tickets to the social. The social goers, once at the hall, buy tickets for booze and for the silent auction prizes, and all the money from the tickets goes to the couple. They recoup the cost of renting the hall and buying the booze and prizes, and they pocket the rest. That's essentially it.

When I park my truck and survey the people getting out of their cars, I notice that everyone is in costume. I am not, mainly because I didn't think that a bunch of grown-ass people would dress up for a Halloween social. I go inside and discover that I am the only fucking person in Dugald Community Club without a fucking costume. There're fairies and dogs and princesses and even two people dressed as the twin towers, and I'm wearing jeans, a hoodie and a baseball shirt.

Shit.

I buy five drink tickets. The witch in green face paint selling the tickets is looking me up and down.

"What are you supposed to be?" she asks.

"I'm not wearing a costume," I say.

"Yeah, you can tell," she says.

Fuck you, witch.

I take my tickets to the bar and exchange one for a warm beer. Budweiser. Fucking hell. I turn from the bar. This girl named Christy I kinda know is standing in front of me dressed as a cat.

"Hey, Brendan," she says. "What are you?"

"I'm a young Noam Chomsky," I say.

"Cool. Who's that?"

"He's a linguist. He's the leading voice of western dissent in the western world. He's great," I say.

"Cool," Christy says.

I sidestep her and make my way towards the dance floor where Shane and Matty and Erica and Chantelle are standing.

"Where's your costume?" Chantelle asks.

"I'm Han Solo," I say. "This is how he dressed when he wasn't flying the Millennium Falcon."

"Sweet," from Shane and Matty.

"Whatever," Chantelle says.

I stand and talk with the CountryGas crew for a while, feeling awkward as the only dipshit who didn't dress up for a Halloween social. My mind drifts and I take in the community club. It seemed so much bigger when I was a kid. I guess it's just me that's gotten bigger. If I were to go across the street and break into my old elementary school, I'd probably feel like a giant.

Man, I should totally break into my old school. That's a great idea.

Nah, I'm too sober for that kind of shit. I use only two of my drink tickets and give the other three away. I'm driving tonight. One DUI was bad enough. Two would be the fucking shits. Best to avoid that.

Late in the night, I'm standing near the DJ booth, on the outer edge of the dance floor. Weird techno music is playing and a strobe light is going. I notice a short figure dressed in dark robes emerge from a group of dancers on the dance floor. It moves very slowly, or maybe it doesn't and it's just a trick the strobe lights are playing on me. As it gets closer, I can see that the short robed figure is wearing a grotesque rubber mask.

If I were on acid right now, I'd be tripping the fuck out. But I'm not. I'm only two beers deep and only slightly concerned about my safety.

The masked figure walks right up to me and motions for me to bend down, and I do.

"Do you know who I am?" I can hear, muffled by the mask and nearly drowned out by techno.

"No," I say.

Carol removes her mask to reveal that it's Carol.

"Oh thank Christ, it's Carol," I say.

Carol says something.

"What?" I say.

She says something else.

"What?" I say again.

She motions for me to bend down to her again.

"Wanna go somewhere to talk?" she asks.

"Sure," I say.

Carol and I leave the community club, cross the street and sit on the swings in the yard of my old school.

"Sorry for being such a downer at my birthday party," Carol says. "I was feeling anti-social or something."

I light a cigarette.

"That happens," I say. "Anti-social ain't such a bad thing. You get too social, and you get what we left back there. A bunch of grown-ass people playing dress up."

"Hey, that can be fun sometimes," Carol says, smiling, holding up her mask.

"I didn't mean you, of course," I say.

I'm smoking, staring through the darkness at my old elementary school. In the fifth grade, I wrote a story, mostly on my own time, called "M.A.P." That stands for Martial Arts Police. The story was about two cops who fought super-villains using kung fu and shit. My teacher liked the story so much that she had me read it in front of the class. My classmates liked it, too. When I was reading that story to them, that was the happiest I'd been since my mom left. I was certain that when I grew up, I would be a professional writer.

When I was in grade six, my teacher, Madame Trudeau, saw me sitting alone writing. She came up to me and said, "Brendan, do you know how much money Stephen King gets per book that he writes?"

I said no. I had no concept of how much adults make for the things they do.

She smiled.

"One million dollars," she said, and she walked away.

I didn't know much, but I knew one million dollars is a lot of money.

I'm brought back to the here and now by Carol touching my leg.

"What're you thinking about?" she asks.

I throw my cigarette butt in the sand.

"You ever feel like your kid self would be really disappointed in the way you turned out?" I ask.

Carol laughs.

"No, I always wanted to be a small-town hotel restaurant waitress," she says.

"What would you like to do most in the world?" I ask.

"I don't know," Carol says. "Travel. See the world a bit before I go to university and start a career. What do you want to do?"

"I kinda want to burn this school to the ground," I say.

Carol laughs again.

"You know what I want to do right now?" she asks.

"What?"

"I kinda want to kiss you," she says.

And then it happens. I don't really have a say in it. Carol's lips are on mine and her hand is still on my leg and her nails are digging in, and then Carol pulls back and then her hands are back in her lap. She's smiling at me.

"Wow," I say.

Carol's name is called from the parking lot of the community club across the street. She looks back.

"Shit," she says. "My ride's leaving. Thanks for hanging out with me."

She gives me a shorter, quicker version of the last kiss, and then she's up from her swing and she's walking back to the parking lot.

"Bye," I say, lighting a new cigarette.

Sitting alone in the dark on a swing in the yard of my old school, I feel bad, and it takes me a while to figure out why I feel so bad. I feel like I just cheated on Anne. But Anne and I aren't in a relationship. We just sleep together, but we don't sleep together. So why do I feel bad? What did I do wrong?

Hmmmmmmmm.

Oh shit. I'm in love with Anne.

CHAPTER 22

Nothing notable happens until almost Christmas. The days and weeks go by like they tend to do. It gets cold and it snows, and pumping gas becomes something you do in a parka and thermal underwear as opposed to something you do in a hoodie and normal underwear. When I'm not at work, I'm at home either sleeping or writing or watching the news as our fighter planes drop bombs on Afghanistan and our troops engage al-Qaeda and the Taliban. Every Wednesday evening I go to writing class, and every Wednesday night I sleep in Anne's bed so that Anne can sleep. On Fridays, George picks me up and we go to Jonas's. Davis and Marc pick up weed from Marc's guy, we go to the bar and the guys pick up girls to take back to Jonas's to smoke dope with. I barely speak to the girls they bring back, and I sit and get drunker and wish I was hanging out with Anne.

Because I'm in love with her.

A week before Christmas, we have our last writing class. Nobody reads anything; we just kind of hang out and eat food that people bring in for a potluck. I can't cook anything much more complex than chicken alfredo, so I bring a fruit platter from the grocery store. Anne brings paper plates and plastic utensils.

"People always forget to bring these things," she says to me, "and then everyone's eating with their hands. It's disgusting. You're welcome."

At one point, I'm talking to the wheelchair man. His name is Carl.

"You're a really good writer, Brendan," he says while eating cake.

"Thanks, man," I say.

"I really enjoyed the stuff you shared."

"I really enjoyed the stuff you shared, too."

This isn't a lie. Carl is a very talented writer.

"You ever think about what you're going to do after this?" he asks.

"Probably go home. I gotta be at the gas station for six," I say.

Carl laughs.

"No. With writing," he says.

I'm silent a moment.

"I haven't really thought about it," I say.

"Well, you should. Talent like yours shouldn't go to waste at a gas station," Carl says.

"Thanks, man," I say. "Good luck with your book."

Carl starts rolling away.

"She likes you, by the way," he says.

"Who?" I say.

With the hand that isn't holding a paper plate full of cake, he points at Anne across the room.

I smile and say, "I hope you're right."

That night, when we get back to Anne's apartment, we don't watch a movie, we don't listen to music and we don't go straight to bed. Anne tells me to stay in the living room, and she goes into her bedroom and comes out with a present poorly wrapped in newspaper.

"This is for you," she says.

I take the present.

"What's this for?" I ask.

"For Christmas, stupid."

"Shit. I didn't get you anything."

"That's okay. You've done a lot for me. That's why I wanted to get you this," she says.

"Thanks," I say, and I unwrap the present. It's new copies of the Distillers' self-titled CD, Alkaline Trio's *From*

Here to Infirmary, Hot Water Music's *A Flight and a Crash* and Rise Against's *The Unraveling.*

"Awesome," I say.

"It's weird that you only listen to Elliott Smith, so I thought I'd broaden your horizons a bit. Elliott Smith is too depressing," Anne says.

I give Anne a hug. Then when we pull away a little, I give her a kiss on the cheek. Then I get brave and I kiss her lips. She lets this happen for a moment, and then she steps back from me.

"What the hell was that?" she says.

"A kiss?" I say.

"Why?"

"'Cause … 'cause I'm in love with you," I say.

Anne looks mad, like she's going to hit me and throw me out of her apartment. But she doesn't. Instead she throws her arms back around me and we're kissing again.

That night, neither of us gets any sleep. It has nothing to do with insomnia.

CHAPTER 23

I go outside to pump gas, but the driver's side door of the car that pulled up opens and the large butch asshole customer gets out and tells me she's going to pump her own gas. I say, "Okay," and then I'm back inside and behind the counter.

The woman pumps $20.01. She comes in to pay, all upset.

"Why does it do that?" she demands.

I'm ringing in her purchase.

"I'm sorry?" I say.

"I pumped exactly twenty dollars. Exactly. When I hung up the nozzle, the price went up one cent. Why does it do that?" the butch woman asks.

"I'm not sure," I say.

"I want to be charged twenty dollars and twenty dollars only," she says.

"That's cool," I say. "Are you paying cash?"

She holds up her debit card. I make a face and I point at our computerized till.

"If you're paying debit, I have to charge you twenty oh one. It's all automated. I really don't have a choice," I say.

The woman scoffs and shakes her head and hands me her debit card.

"So who gets the extra penny?" she asks. "How many times does this happen a day? Who's cashing in on this?"

I look back at Shane as I'm doing the transaction. He just smiles at me. When the receipt prints I hand it to the woman. I also give her a penny from the take-a-penny-leave-a-penny tray.

"Here," I say. "Now you paid only twenty dollars. Cool?"

The butch woman doesn't take the penny. She makes a pissed-off face.

"What the fuck am I going to do with a penny?" she says. She leaves.

I turn back to Shane and laugh.

"All that over a penny," I say.

Shane's looking at me weird.

"What's wrong with you today?" he asks.

"What?"

"I've seen you lose your shit over less than the bullshit that woman was serving you. You're laughing and making jokes and shit. What the hell? What's up with you today?"

I smile.

"I had a good night last night," I say.

Shane's smiling, too.

"You got laid," he says.

"No."

"Sure you did."

"No, I didn't."

"That's the only thing that explains this."

"You're wrong."

"Who was it? The waitress?"

"Fuck off."

A car pulls up, and I bolt out the door, as fast as a human can. I don't like talking about sex. It makes me uncomfortable. I'm kind of a prude in that respect. I don't really talk about sex; I don't really make sexual jokes. I like to think I'm a gentleman. That's a rare thing in this day and age. I just think that that which is done behind closed doors should remain behind closed doors. I think that's what upset me most about the whole Marissa disaster. When I found out about her, suddenly I was talking about my sex life to sympathetic female co-workers and I felt really awful about it.

I guess I'm just a private person.

When I get home from work, I try to nap but I can't stop thinking about Anne and our nice night last night. I put Alkaline Trio on my stereo, and I lie on top of my covers and think about how nice it'll be to see Anne at the next class.

Oh shit. There are no more classes. Yesterday was the last one.

Oh shit. I have no way of communicating with Anne. I don't have her phone number. I don't have her e-mail. All I know is where she lives.

Fuck. I'm going to turn into a stalker, aren't I?

CHAPTER 24

On Tuesday, I sleep in till noon, the usual time that I'd be getting off work, but I don't work today 'cause it's Christmas.

I put on an old pair of jeans and an old T-shirt, and then I'm downstairs in the living room. Dad's watching the History Channel. Spitfires are shooting down Nazis.

"Afternoon," my dad says. He always says that instead of *Good morning* if I wake up past a time he deems acceptable.

"Hey," I say.

"It's Christmas," he says.

"It is."

My dad produces two cartons of Export Gold cigarettes and hands them to me.

"Merry Christmas," he says. "I thought you'd probably enjoy these more than some other goddamn thing."

I smile.

"Thanks," I say. "This is great. This is very John Hughes of you."

My dad looks confused sitting on the couch.

"Who?"

"John Hughes. He wrote and directed *The Breakfast Club*. One of the characters in the movie gets a carton of smokes from his dad for Christmas," I say.

My dad looks like he's having a hard time holding back his anger.

"I'm trying to do a nice thing here," he says.

"I know. I'm sorry. This is really great. Thank you," I say, then I run upstairs and put away my cigarettes and I grab the bottle of Crown Royal I got my dad for Christmas. I head back downstairs and hand it to him. He seems to like it.

He produces an envelope.

"This came for you, too," he says.

It's a card from my mom, wishing me a merry Christmas. There's a cheque for five hundred dollars. I close the card quickly so my dad doesn't see the cheque. It would just piss him off. I make a mental note to throw the money into my savings account when the credit union opens again after the holidays.

"What should we have for dinner tonight?" my dad asks, turning his attention back to the World War Two violence on the TV screen.

"We have chicken," I say. "That's kinda like turkey."

"Sounds good."

I sit in the chair beside the couch and watch the History Channel with my dad for a while until I start niccing out, and then I go outside into the cold for a Christmas smoke.

CHAPTER 25

It's been almost two weeks since I last saw Anne, since we had sex. I decide that she's as stressed out as I am at the fact that we have no way of communicating, so I psych myself up and after work drive into the city and park on Anne's street in front of her building. And I wait. I'm about to give up and go home when I see Anne walking up the sidewalk. I get out of the truck.

"Hey," I say to her.

"What are you doing here?" she asks.

Shit. That's not the reaction I was hoping for.

"I wanted to see you and I had no way of getting in touch with you so I thought I'd pop by," I say.

Anne looks put off, but she also looks really tired. We're standing in front of the entrance to her building. She's making no attempt to unlock the door, so I figure she's not planning to invite me up. She just stands staring at me.

"I'm sorry. This was a bad idea," I say.

I turn and head back to my truck. I stop halfway across the street when Anne calls out to me.

"Brendan," she says. "Come pick me up at nine, 'kay?"

I turn around just in time to see Anne disappear into her building. I get into my truck and I drive to Transcona, to the Burger Factory. I order a burger and fries. I sit by myself and eat slowly, killing time. Then I'm slowly drinking my Coke. Then I refill it. When it gets close to nine, I'm back in my truck and at Anne's apartment again. At nine o'clock sharp, she comes out of the building and gets into the truck. We drive to Portage, to our little café. Anne orders black coffee and since my stomach is so full from the Burger Factory, I just get a glass of water.

"So what's going on, Anne?" I ask, lighting a cigarette.

She lights one, too.

"I'm sorry I was a bit of a bitch earlier," she says. "I didn't mean to be. This is just a little difficult ... because of the age difference."

"It didn't bother you before."

"We were just hanging out before."

"I was sleeping in your bed."

"Yeah, but we weren't *sleeping together.* Now we are."

I smile.

"Sleeping together? Not 'We slept together'?" I say.

Anne shakes her head.

"You're such a child," she says. "This is what I'm talking about. You're seven years younger than me. You're fucking twenty. I'm almost fucking thirty. Can you see how this is difficult for me?"

I ash my cigarette.

"So what do you want to do?" I ask.

"I want to be in a mature relationship," Anne says.

"And you can't have that with me?"

"No, idiot, I want that with you."

"So what's the problem?"

Anne slumps back in her seat.

"My friends are going to make fun of me," she says.

We both sit looking at each other for a moment. Then we start laughing.

That night, in Anne's bed, we're kissing. When I put my hand on her thigh, she pulls away.

"No sex tonight, 'kay?" she says.

"Okay," I say.

"It's just not a good time, okay?"

"That's cool. Lady stuff?"

"What? Oh. Yeah. I've got lady stuff."

"That's cool. I just like being with you," I say.

Anne smiles one of her rare genuine smiles and we kiss some more, and when I settle down to sleep and the lights go out, I fall asleep with a grin on my face.

CHAPTER 26

It's Friday evening and I'm standing with Davis in the dirty kitchen of some upstairs apartment in the heart of Transcona. Sitting at the kitchen table chopping lines of coke is Marc's drug dealer, an Eminem-looking motherfucker with bleached-blond hair and a dirty wife beater. Marc isn't with us. He had to go pick up some girls to come with us to the Oak tonight, so he put Davis and me in charge of picking up drugs.

I feel slightly uncomfortable.

Marc's drug dealer, JT, snorts a line off his dirty kitchen table, then turns to Davis and me.

"I'm out of pot. I ain't got shit," he tells us. "I've got a fuckload of coke, though."

"Well, that sucks," I say.

JT motions to his remaining chopped lines.

"Do you partake?" he asks.

I wave a dismissive hand. I haven't smoked pot since the night at Jonas's when I threw up. I'm not particularly eager to see how cocaine is going to affect me.

"Sure," Davis says.

He takes JT's rolled-up twenty, bends down and snorts hard.

When he stands up straight again, Davis looks like he's going to sneeze. He's all bug eyed. Instead of sneezing (which would be funny), he repeats the word *wow* several times.

JT points the rolled-up twenty at me.

"You're up," he says.

I take a five out of my own wallet and roll it up while looking JT straight in the eyes. Beside me, Davis is still alive, so fuck it. I bend down and snort a line of cocaine. I stand up straight.

No effect. I wait longer. I don't really feel anything. I guess there's probably some kind of delay. All I feel is this disgusting medicinal drip in the back of my throat, like I just snorted a line of Tylenol. It makes me sniff uncontrollably. Davis is doing the same.

"Awesome, huh?" he says.

I turn and smile. "Yeah."

JT hands Davis a small bag.

"Here you guys go," he says. "Have fun tonight. No charge."

Davis puts the bag in his pocket and tells JT to stop by Jonas's later tonight to "party." JT says he will, and then he's back to snorting lines off his dirty kitchen table, and Davis and I are gone.

When we get back to Jonas's, Marc is there with three girls I've never met before. Emphasis on *girls*.

"How old are they?" I ask him.

"It's okay," he says. "They're sixteen."

That's not okay.

"How are they coming to the bar with us?" I ask.

"They've got their sisters' IDs," he says. "It's cool."

"It's cool for you and Jonas. You guys are eighteen. Me and George and Davis are twenty, man. We can't be sneaking sixteen-fucking-year-old girls into bars," I say.

"You won't be," he says. "Jonas and I will."

Marc smiles and pats me on the back and heads into the kitchen. I follow. The girls are sitting at the kitchen table, and Davis has the bag of coke out and he's showing everybody. Everybody looks really excited. I take out a cigarette and duck out into the garage and light it. George is smoking, too.

"How do you feel about all this?" I ask him.

"The coke or the underage girls?"

"Or both."

"I think this night has the potential to go very bad," he says. "So I'm going to get really drunk and dissociate myself from all of it."

I smile.

"Good plan," I say.

And that's what we do. We go to the bar and get drunk, and then when we head back to Jonas's and everyone's snorting coke and acting stupid, we get drunker. When JT and his drugged-out hooker of a girlfriend show up with more coke, we get drunker still. At four in the morning, when I'm in the living room and I look over and see JT putting little white rocks into a pipe and smoking them, I find my way to the basement to a couch and I pass out.

Fuck this shit.

CHAPTER 27

This morning, we get a delivery of product and shit, so while Shane is pumping gas I stock the shelves with new shit or I store the new shit in the back depending on whether it's needed in the store yet or not. Some of the boxes are full of bottles of gas-line antifreeze, and Jane asks me to make a display of it. Right next to the entrance, I stack four of the boxes on top of each other. Then I open up another box and I stand the bottles of antifreeze from the opened box on top of the top stacked box. Display done.

Later in the shift, I'm behind the counter when an asshole customer comes in wearing a suit and long coat. He notices my antifreeze display and chuckles to himself.

He walks over to the counter and places his gold credit card on it. I look up from the card to the asshole customer.

"You know," he says, "you'd sell more of that stuff if the labels on the bottles were facing the customers when they walk in."

I look at my display. The bottles are turned the way they ended up when I quickly stood them on the stacked boxes. I didn't really put much effort into making sure all the labels were facing the same way, 'cause that's insane.

"Most people know what a bottle of gas-line antifreeze looks like by the bottle," I say. "They don't need to read the label."

The man smiles.

"You'd be surprised," he says. "Most people can be pretty stupid. I know. I'm in marketing."

The asshole customer taps his gold card on the counter.

Fucking barf.

Shane comes back in from the cold and the gold card transaction gets done and Mr. Marketing is on his way. At the end of my shift, I find myself in Jane's little office in the back.

"Brendan, do you want to switch shifts with Matty?" she asks me.

"Sure," I say. "When does he want to switch?"

"He wants to switch permanently," she says. "You'd be working the noon to six shift, and he'd be working in the morning with Shane."

Not having to get up at five in the morning every day sounds pretty nice.

"Who'd I be working with?" I ask.

"You'd be working with Chantelle Mondays, Wednesdays and Fridays, and with Erica Tuesdays and Thursdays. And Heidi works the cover shift between four and seven. How's that sound?" Jane asks.

Working with Heidi? Fuck yeah!

"Sounds good," I say.

Jane smiles.

"Great. I'll change the schedule, then," she says.

I thank Jane, and then I'm outside lighting a cigarette. Shane comes out of the store.

"This was our last shift together," I tell him.

"Did you get fired?" he asks.

"No, I'm working the afternoon shift starting Monday. You'll be working with Matty now," I say.

"Oh. You wanna go for lunch?"

"I could eat. Sure."

"Cool."

And so Shane and I go to the hotel restaurant and have lunch and some beers to celebrate our last shift together. After lunch, I walk home in the cold, smoking cigarettes to keep warm. I nap when I get home, then I shower and eat dinner, then I'm in George's truck when he shows up at six and we're bombing it into the city.

At the Oak, I get a nice surprise. My friend Ryan is here. Ryan used to play lead guitar in Lost Astronaut. A few months ago, Ryan was kicked out of the band for reasons that were never made clear to me. Ryan was out and Marc took over lead guitar duties, in addition to being frontman of the band. Apparently, when you get kicked out of a band, you stop being friends with your old bandmates, too, 'cause I haven't seen Ryan since all this went down.

Ryan is the most positive person I've ever met. The man is always smiling. He has the word *YES* tattooed on his arm. When he got it done, I asked him, "Why'd you get *YES* tattooed on your arm?" He told me, "'Cause yes is better than no."

Top-notch guy.

Ryan gives me a vigorous handshake when he sees me that includes a slap on the back. He's smiling, naturally, and that makes me smile.

"How's it going, buddy?" I ask.

"Great, man. Just perfect," he says. "You?"

"I'm living. What've you been up to?"

"Making music, brother. Making beautiful music."

"Yeah?"

"Yeah. I started a new band."

"Cool. What're you called?"

"The One-Eyed Jacks."

"Nice. What do you play?"

"Good old rock 'n' roll, brother. Good old rock 'n' roll."

Ryan's attention is stolen away by a pretty girl that I assume is his new girlfriend. I stand drinking my beer for a little while, but when Ryan doesn't turn back to me, I pat him on the shoulder and tell him it was nice seeing him, and then I'm gone.

After the bar, I'm walking on the snowy sidewalk in the cold with George and Jonas and Davis and Marc and a random handful of people from the bar who're coming back to Jonas's to do blow with us. I'm walking next to Marc.

"I saw you talking to Ryan," he says.

"Yeah," I say.

"How's he doing?"

"He's doing really good."

"Was he trying to get back into the band?"

"Huh?"

"Did he ask you to ask me to let him back into the band?"

"No. He was actually saying he started a new band."

Marc laughs.

"I bet they're fucking terrible," he says.

I walk the rest of the way in silence.

CHAPTER 28

I walk through the door into Anne's apartment. I'm about to throw my jacket on the floor, but I don't. The apartment is cleaner than I've ever seen it. I can see into the living room area, and Anne's coffee table is cleared off and there're bowls of chips and plates with fruits and vegetables on it. Anne is sitting on the couch, drinking wine. She gets up and takes my jacket from me.

"I'm going to throw this on the bed," she says, and she does.

When she comes back from the bedroom, I ask, "What's going on?"

Anne smiles.

"I've been nervous about us possibly running into my friends when we're out in the world —"

"Is that why we always hang out here?"

"— so I decided to do a little immersion therapy. I invited all my friends over tonight to meet you. We're getting all this over with in one shot —"

"Like taking off a Band-Aid?"

"— so I can finally get over this block I have, this awful feeling that you're too young for me and everyone is going to ostracize me for robbing the cradle. It's all in my head, I know, so when my friends get here and see how great you are and they all like you as much as I like you, then it will all be over and I can get over it, y'know?" Anne says.

"If you were a guy and I were a girl, this wouldn't even be an issue," I say.

Anne looks angry.

"Don't lump me in with those assholes who chase after girls seven years younger than they are," she says.

I'm about to respond, but Anne's buzzer buzzes. She walks over to it.

"There's beer in the fridge," she tells me before she says into the intercom, "Come on up."

Anne's worries prove to be baseless. I get along great with her friends. I'm funny and witty and great to be around, and so are her friends. No one asks me about my age, presumably because I don't look any younger than anyone else at the party. I feel very at ease with Anne's friends. I'm tipsy and I'm happy that no one's cutting lines on the coffee table. It's nice for a change.

Later in the night, I'm standing in the kitchen with a guy named Cole who seems pretty cool. He's got a shaved head and traditional tattoos on his arms.

"So, how'd you and Anne meet?" he asks me.

"We were in the same writing workshop class at the U of W," I tell him.

"You're a writer?"

"Trying to be."

"What do you write?"

"Different stuff, I guess. After Columbine, I wrote a novel about a school shooting," I say.

"Cool. You try to get it published?"

"I tried for a little while. I sent out some stuff, but then I got discouraged."

"Ain't that the bitch of it," Cole says. "You ever think about self-publishing?"

"No. I wouldn't know where to start."

"It's easier than you'd think. There're some websites that'll help you through it. Watch out for the scammers, though," he says.

I smile.

"When I was a kid, like ten or so, my favourite thing in the world was going to the stationary store in the town where I grew up and buying these little pads of paper. I'd take them home and write these serialized stories all about this guy who had to fight all these different kinds of super-villains. I wrote dozens and dozens of these stories, and when I was done one, I'd tear it off the pad and staple the pages together and I'd draw the cover art and I'd keep all these little stories in one of the drawers that was part of my bed. That was my favourite thing in the world when I was a kid," I say.

"Cool," Cole says. "Do you still have the stories?"

I'm not smiling anymore.

"Nah. I didn't have a whole lot of support from people for my writing when I was younger. I remember one day I was looking at all my little stories and I was thinking about all the time I wasted writing them, so I threw them all in the garbage," I say.

"Bummer."

"Yeah."

"You should write them again," Cole says.

I make a face.

"Nah. That was kid stuff," I say.

"So update it," he says. "You said it was your favourite thing to do. If it brought you joy then, maybe it will now, too."

"You want another beer?" I ask.

"Sure."

I open the fridge and grab us fresh beers.

"How'd you meet Anne?" I ask.

"We were in CreComm together," he says.

I'm staring at my new friend blankly.

"What's that?" I ask.

"Creative Communications."

"And that is?"

"Anne's never told you about what she took in college?"

"Anne still hasn't told me what she does for work."

"She's an advertising copywriter."

"So she copyrights stuff?"

"She writes copy. She writes ads."

"Oh. Cool. And she got that job 'cause she took Creative Communications in college?" I ask.

"Yes. At Red River."

"Cool."

"You ever think of taking the course?" Cole asks me.

"Considering I've just heard of it, no, I haven't," I say. "What is it?"

He laughs.

"It's training for writing in journalism, advertising and public relations," he says.

"Cool. So what do you do?"

"I'm a print journalist. I work for the *Free Press*," he says.

My eyes get wide.

"You ever see the movie *The Paper?*" I ask.

"Fuck yeah. That movie rules," Cole says.

I hang out with Cole most of the night. All the guests leave by three o'clock. When Anne is seeing one of her girlfriends out, the girlfriend drunkenly points at me and tells Anne, "I like this one much better than Richard." I don't think much of this.

Anne and I are in bed by three thirty.

"How come you've never told me you're an advertising copywriter?" I ask her.

"I don't like talking about work when I'm not at work," she says.

"Was Creative Communications fun?"

"It was a lot of fun," she says. "Most of the friends I have now I made while in CreComm."

"Do you think I would like it?"

Anne turns to look at me directly.

"Are you interested in the program?" she asks.

"It sounds like I'd like it," I say.

"It's really hard to get in, but I could coach you if you really want it," she says.

"I really want it," I say. "I want a job where I write for a living."

"Cool. Remind me in the morning. I'm really drunk," Anne says, and then she turns out the lamp next to her.

CHAPTER 29

Monday morning, I'm woken up by my dad pounding his fist on my bedroom door.

"What!?!" I yell, my throat dry and my voice hoarse.

"You going to work today? It's five thirty," I hear him shout from the hallway.

"No."

"Why not?"

"I don't work at six this morning. I work at noon."

Silence for a moment.

"Well, how'm I supposed to know that?" he says.

I calm down a bit. I know he's just trying to help me out.

"Have a good day, Dad," I say.

"You too," he says. Then I hear his work boots clomping down the hall back towards the kitchen. A minute later I hear the back door open, close and lock. There's silence again.

I try to go back to sleep, and I suppose I do, but it's that I've-already-been-awake-and-now-I'm-trying-to-sleep-but-I'm-not-really-tired-I-just-don't-want-to-wake-up sleep. By ten o'clock, I'm out of bed and in the kitchen making eggs and bacon. My dad's little TV on top of the fridge is on, and I've got it tuned to the twenty-four–hour news channel. I watch the well-put-together news people in their nice clothes talk sternly and seriously about terrorism and crime, and I think, How great would it be to be one of them? Just telling stories for a living. That's all they're doing. Just relaying facts to the viewers so they may make informed decisions on the things that matter most to them, that matter most to their community, their city, their country and their world. There's honour in that. There's integrity in that. Being a journalist is a noble profession. And man, what a great time to get into the business. With all the 9/11-related bullshit going on, journalism is having a fucking boom. I know, it's gross, professionals benefiting from all the awful shit going on in the world, but that awful shit is going to happen whether I'm there to point a camera or a mic at it or not. Why not make a living from transforming that awful shit into a news story, beaming it up into space and back down from satellites to millions of viewers' homes? People want to know, and I'm going to tell them.

If I could present it to my dad like that when I tell him I'm trying out for Creative Communications, I think he'd be on board. He'd realize that I feel strongly about this and he'd be happy that I wouldn't have to spend my life building walls like he does until my back or knees inevitably give out.

Yeah. He'd give me his full blessing.

Yeah, fucking right.

After my breakfast I hop in the shower so I'll smell nice for the first hour of my shift before I start smelling like gas and grease. I walk to work in the cold, smoking cigarettes. I like smoking in the cold. The smoke mixes with the condensed breath coming out of your lungs and forms a giant cloud. It's like you've got a fire inside you, a volcano whose eruptions only you control. It's fun.

I get to the station ten minutes before my shift. Chantelle is already there. Shane and Matty are just finishing their shift. They're laughing and having fun, as friends who've just spent six hours getting paid to hang out would. This kinda makes me feel a little lousy. Shane is clearly having more fun with Matty than he ever did with me. Matty's a fun guy with a great sense of humour. All I ever did was bitch about the asshole customers and read the newspapers and bitch about the news. I must've been a real bummer to work with.

But I would take working with a bummer like me over working with Chantelle any day. I've never worked with her before, and I never noticed when we would all hang out and drink together at the Oakbank Bar, but Chantelle is kind of a shitty person. She's dumb and close-minded and opinionated, and really arrogant with her dumb, close-minded opinions. We establish early on that I'm going to do gas for the whole shift and she's going to work the store for the whole shift, which is fine by me, but every time one of her girlfriends comes in (which is often) she drops everything to stand and gossip with them, like she's still in high school. I guess, since she's only eighteen, high school isn't all that far off for her. She gets personal calls on the station's phone, too, and she'll just stand and have a conversation on the phone while I do transactions, keeping an eye on the pumps for cars that pull up. And when cars do pull up and I tell her I've got to go outside to, y'know, do my job, she makes a face like I'm inconveniencing her and only then does she do her job, but with a bitchy attitude. Sure, I hate the asshole customers, but I'm at least diplomatic with them. I try to be accommodating to their insanity, and I wait till after they're gone to talk shit about them. Chantelle is rude to their faces.

And she's rude to me, too. Every time I come in from pumping gas, she says that something stinks. Every time. I ask her, "What does it smell like?" She can't tell me. She just keeps saying something stinks. When I come in from outside. When I come out of the bathroom, even just from peeing. When I come out of the cooler after restocking it. Always. Always something stinks.

There's no gas right now. I'm sitting on the little ladder while Chantelle helps a customer. When he leaves, Chantelle turns to me.

"His hands were shaking," she says. "Why would his hands be shaking?"

I stare at her a moment.

"Maybe you make him nervous," I say.

"He didn't seem nervous."

"You sold him cigarettes. Maybe he was niccing out."

"Why would that make your hands shake?"

"It does sometimes."

"I think he was fucked in the head."

"Maybe. Or maybe he narrowly missed getting into an accident on his way home from work and his adrenalin is still going. Or maybe he just got into a big argument with his wife and he needed a smoke to calm down. Maybe he has MS or Parkinson's. Maybe he thinks you're pretty. Or maybe, y'know, it's late January and he's just fucking cold," I say.

"Jeez," Chantelle says. "Sorry I said anything."

I turn my head and stare out the window, wondering why the hell I agreed to switch my schedule. There's silence in the store for a few minutes until Heidi walks in at four for the cover shift. I'm so happy to see her, I just about jump up and hug her.

"How was school?" I ask her.

"Awful. One day I'm going to blow up Oakbank Collegiate," she says.

"I loved high school," Chantelle says.

"I bet you did," Heidi says, then turns to me. "I hear you're done with your cleanse."

"Sure am."

She pulls a burnt CD out of her backpack.

"I burnt you some Ryan Adams," she says.

"Sweet."

Heidi motions to the CD player/radio.

"Throw it on," she says.

"We're listening to Hot 103," Chantelle says.

"Majority rules," I say, and I put on the CD.

And the last two hours of my shift are much nicer.

CHAPTER 30

The next day, I start working with Erica. Erica is tall. At the least, she's six feet. She's thin and beautiful and has long blonde hair. She's essentially a human Barbie doll. If you're into that sort of thing, she's your perfect woman. I am not into that sort of thing. I'm into the opposite of that sort of thing. I think that a lot of guys would be nervous having to spend an entire shift talking to Erica. Since I'm not attracted to her in the slightest, I've got no problem with it. Ten Ericas wouldn't come close to being as attractive as one Anne.

Erica is the opposite of Chantelle, personality-wise. She's genuinely nice, she's hard working, she's great with the customers, she has a great sense of humour and she insists on doing her fair share of the gas duties. When Heidi arrives at four, Erica doesn't say anything when the CD player gets commandeered. We all have a great time working together until Erica's and my shift ends at six.

I decide that Tuesdays and Thursdays with Erica and Heidi are going to be much more tolerable than Mondays, Wednesdays and Fridays with Heidi and Bitchface.

CHAPTER 31

Weeks go by. When I'm not at the gas station during the week, during the day, I'm at home preparing for getting into CreComm. Anne has been coaching me. First it was the aptitude test. Anne told me what to expect on it. One morning I went in to Red River's Notre Dame campus and sat in a classroom full of other hopefuls, and we wrote a test that was exactly as Anne said it would be. It was multiple choice. Who is Quebec's Premier? Which is not one of the Great Lakes? Who of the below listed is not a legitimate journalist? Which of the below is not an African nation? Shit like that.

Two weeks after the test, I got a letter saying I had advanced to the next stage, which involves submitting a portfolio of my writing. I gathered some of my best stuff together and added a few op-ed–type pieces to highlight my journalistic skills. Anne looked it all over, gave me the thumbs up and encouraged me to submit what I had. That was two weeks ago. I haven't heard anything since.

I still hang out every Friday night at Jonas's. Every night with the Lost Astronaut guys was pretty much the same, like the background in a Flintstones cartoon repeating over and over. We meet at the house. Davis and Marc go pick up pot and coke that we all chip in for, even though I do not indulge. We go to the bar, the guys tell girls at the bar about the drugs we've got back at the house and by the end of the night a small horde is following us from the bar to Jonas's. I get stupid fucking drunker and pass out in some quiet dark corner somewhere while the party rages on through the night, fuelled by cocaine. Sometimes people are still partying when George and I leave in the morning to go get breakfast.

Saturdays I spend with Anne. It's not the only day when I'm with her. I'm over at her apartment all the time. Saturday's just our date night. After being accepted by her friends, I found that Anne was more inclined to go out in public with me. We branched out from going for coffee to going out to semi-nice restaurants, going to movies, even just going for walks. It's nice.

I don't let myself think about Anne when I'm not with

her. If my experience with Marissa taught me anything, it's that a relationship can go sour really fast. Like Millennium Falcon fast. I thought things were going fine with Marissa one day, and the next I found out she was sleeping with other guys. Acting like a love-struck idiot when you're in a new relationship just sets you up for a fall. Anne and I could break up in two months, or we could get married. I have no idea. I'll get excited when it's time to get excited, like when I'm picking out my tux. Until then, I'm going to stay rational.

I do like her a lot, though.

Shit. I've said too much.

CHAPTER 32

Spring is coming and the snow is melting, so I dart outside to pump gas in just a hoodie (and jeans, obviously). The vehicle in need of gas is an older Dodge Caravan that's substantially rusted. The frumpy school teacher/vice-principal/librarian-looking woman in the driver's seat tells me to fill the tank. I get it started, and then I wash her windows and headlights. When I'm back at the pump, the woman gets out of her van.

"I think winter might be over," she says.

"Yep," I say with a smile.

"Thank God," she says and laughs.

I nod.

"Do you like movies?" she asks.

I'm not getting a flirtatious vibe from this woman. I'm sure she's not going to ask me out on a date, so I'm intrigued to see where this is going.

"Yeah, I love movies," I say.

"Have you seen *Left Behind?*"

"No, but I've heard of it. Kirk Cameron? From *Growing Pains?* It's a movie about the apocalypse, right?" I say.

"Yes. Based on Tim LaHaye and Jerry B. Jenkins's books. So you've heard of it?" she says.

"Yeah. I think I saw something about it on the Internet. Sounded interesting. I love stuff about the Armageddon and shit," I say.

The nozzle clicks off. I top off the woman's gas and hang up the nozzle and the woman follows me into the store. Chantelle is on the phone so I do the transaction myself. The woman shakes my hand when I hand her the receipt.

"My name is Mary," she says.

Of course it is.

"Brendan," I say.

"Nice to meet you, Brendan," she says. "I really recommend *Left Behind.* You should see it."

"I'll keep it in mind."

"Take care, Brendan."

"You too."

Chantelle is off the phone.

"What was that all about?" she says in her stupid bitch voice.

"Don't worry about it," I say.

After work, George picks me up, and the machinery of another boring Friday night is set in motion. This Friday plays out like every other, the only deviation being that Ryan is at the bar again. Talking to him is the only interesting part of the night, because it's the only curveball from a pitcher that habitually throws fastballs.

"Are you having fun?" I ask George as he drives us back to Oakbank the next morning.

"What do you mean?"

"We do the same fucking thing ever Friday night. Don't you think it's getting boring?"

"What else do you have in mind?"

I'm quiet a moment.

"I don't know. Anything else."

"That's not very specific."

"It feels like we're in a rut."

"The other guys are having the time of their lives."

"Then it's just me in the rut. Going to the same bar and hitting on the same girls and doing a bunch of drugs is not my vision of the time of my life," I say.

Now George is quiet a moment.

"I hear ya. The problem is, at our age, this is what we do. We go to bars. We hit on girls. We get drunk. We do drugs. If it makes you feel better, it's just a phase," he says.

"Yeah?"

"Yeah. In five or ten years you're going to be married with kids and a mortgage, and you're going to hate life for horrifying new reasons," he says.

We both laugh, drowning out Motorhead coming out of the truck's speakers.

That night I'm on Anne's couch watching a movie. I'm sitting upright and Anne is lying, resting against my side, her head on my shoulder. Now that I'm staying the night more often, now that we're in a relationship, Anne seems less frazzled. She's sleeping better and it's doing her a world of good. She doesn't get as frustrated with me as she did when we first met. She's putting on weight. She's not as thin as she was months ago, leading me to believe she wasn't lying when she said she was curvy before the insomnia set in. The way she's lying on me, I can see down her V-neck and I can see definite cleavage. I look away so as not to get a boner. We're watching *Taxi Driver*. Anne might think it's weird that I'm getting sexually aroused while a mohawked Travis Bickle lays waste to a bunch of pimps and johns.

Robert DeNiro and Cybill Shepard are reunited in the taxicab, and the credits roll. Anne stands and ejects the disc and turns off the TV.

"Not the most romantic movie, but I fucking love it," she says.

I'm smiling up at her.

"What?"

"You're beautiful," I say.

Anne makes an unimpressed face.

"Awww, you think I'm beautiful?" she says, putting on a bimbo voice.

"No, you are beautiful. What I think has nothing to do with it," I say.

Anne stares at me for a moment, unreadable. She sits next to me.

"I think you're beautiful, too. In a man way," she says.

"Thanks."

"You are. You're tall, dark and handsome. Women love that shit."

"Yeah, right."

Anne's hand goes to my lap.

"You have a big dick, too," she says.

I cross my leg over my knee, and she pulls her hand away.

"You don't have to say shit like that to me," I say.

"What shit?"

"You don't have to lie to me to make me feel better. I'm okay with it."

"Okay with what?"

"I know I don't have a big dick. It's fine. I'm fine with it. It doesn't make me feel bad, but you lying about it makes me feel bad," I say.

"Where is this coming from?" Anne asks.

I let out a long sigh.

"I was kinda with this girl a little while ago, sort of, and we had slept together, and then we were at the bar in Oakbank. For some reason I had a little twenty pack of cigarettes and she had a normal twenty-five pack and I pushed my pack next to hers and I said, 'My pack is smaller and cuter than yours.' And she said, 'Yeah, your cigarette package is small, just like the package between your legs,'" I say.

"What a jerk."

"Whatever," I say. "A couple weeks later, I found out she was sleeping with other guys. I imagine they had more to offer her in that department."

Anne touches my cheek.

"Brendan, you do not have a small penis. I can't comprehend how you could think that. Your penis is the perfect size. Seriously. It's not too big. It's not too small. It's perfect. Women who want giant porn-star dicks in them, in my opinion, often have cavernous, flappitty vaginas. They're the female equivalent of guys who think giant, fake, Frankenboobs are hot. Fuck those people. It's all so fake and revolting. We have amazing sex because we fit each other perfectly. If you had a giant cock, it wouldn't be enjoyable for me. It would hurt. You don't want to inflict pain on your partner. Sex is supposed to feel good, and with you it feels really good. You shouldn't feel inadequate to anyone. It should be the other way around," Anne says.

Needless to say, Anne and I had sex shortly after this conversation.

CHAPTER 33

On Monday, I have an interview at Red River College's Princess Street Campus. It's the last stage of my entrance process. If I pass this, I'll be going to school in the fall.

I'm sitting in a tiny, cluttered office. There's a small, serious-looking woman in front of me and beside me is a small Indian man who says nothing. The woman is asking me questions.

First, she asks me if I feel the front page of today's issue of the *Free Press* is biased. Anne gave me the heads up on this. She told me they'd ask about the paper, so before I left the house this morning, I made sure to memorize the front page. I recall that the picture on the front was of a man holding up a framed photo of his mother, who died in a hospital waiting room waiting for treatment.

I tell my interviewer that I do, in fact, think there was a bias.

Satisfied, the woman asks me why I want to be a CreCommer. I tell her that I want to make a living from writing, that my ultimate goal is to become a journalist and a professional novelist. She tells me that I should have more practical goals, that becoming a professional novelist is very difficult. She asks me if I'm familiar with certain local authors. She asks me what I think of their work.

"Right now, I'm mostly reading books that I hear about from movies, like *Fight Club*, *High Fidelity* and *Bringing Out the Dead*," I say.

The questions continue. I'm given about ten seconds to answer, and then the woman cuts me off by asking another question. I look over at the small Indian man beside me. He's still not saying anything. He's just writing stuff. He doesn't even look at me.

They're trying to make me angry, I realize. They're trying to rattle me.

The woman asks another question, but instead of answering right away, I reach into the breast pocket of my dress shirt and I remove a package of mints. I take one of the mint lozenges out of the pack, then unwrap its individual wrapper and pop the mint into my mouth.

I place the package and the empty wrapper back in my pocket. I look at the interviewer and my non-interviewer. They both have what-the-fuck? looks on their faces.

"I'm sorry. What was your question?" I say, smiling.

The interview resumes.

CHAPTER 34

The woman in the car is gorgeous. She has dyed black hair and blue eyes and her skin is pale white. She looks like Anne. They could be sisters. She hands me a twenty for her gas. Then she gives me a loonie.

I try giving the dollar back to her.

"Your gas was only twenty dollars," I remind her.

She smiles and laughs nervously.

"It's your tip," she says.

"Thanks, but you don't have to do that."

"No, but I want to. I'm a server. It's ridiculous that we get tips and you guys don't. So there. I'm tipping you. We're both in the service industry. Solidarity," she says.

"Thanks," I say. "I'll buy a chocolate bar."

"Enjoy it," she says, and she drives away.

I go inside and show Heidi my tip.

"Why'd you get a tip?" Chantelle asks in her bitch voice.

"'Cause I'm awesome," I say over my shoulder to her. Then to Heidi I say, "Not bad, huh?"

"That's awesome," she says. "Imagine, if we got a dollar tip from every car that we served, we'd be rich in no time."

Chantelle laughs and says, "Keep dreaming."

Chantelle lives with her parents in a big house on a huge lot in the country. She has fucking horses. She forgets that it's her parents who are rich, not Chantelle. She's a university student who works part time in a CountryGas station.

I move to the chocolate bar and chips aisle and grab a Snickers. Heidi rings me through.

"You get a tip and you spend it right away? Nice," Chantelle says.

"Yeah, I was going to put it in a high-yield bond, but I'm kinda hungry," I say.

"Whatever," says Chantelle.

CHAPTER 35

Early in my time on the afternoon shift, I develop a new favourite customer. Well, customers. There're two of them, and I would never dream of calling them assholes. They are the sweetest people on the planet. They're an elderly Irish couple, and every afternoon at about three o'clock they come in to validate their scratch tickets and buy more. I imagine that their visit to CountryGas is part of a walk the two take together every day.

Fucking hell. I can't wait to be retired.

Even Chantelle is nice to them. It's impossible not to be. She chats with them while she scans their lotto tickets, and I sit on the ladder watching for gas customers. Chantelle is telling the elderly couple about a trip she took to England once. I make a mental note to explain to her the faux pas of confusing Irish people for English people. To restore their faith in young people, as the couple is walking out, I get their attention.

"I'm half Irish," I say.

The man smiles and his blue eyes sparkle.

"What's your name?" he asks.

"Brendan McCaughan," I say.

"That's a great name," he says. "You don't look Irish."

"I'm Italian on my mom's side."

"What's your mother's maiden name?"

"Votolato."

"That's a great name, too."

The woman is smiling at me.

"You could be one of the Black Irish," she says.

"Cool," I say.

They tell me to take care, and then they're off on the second half of their walk.

Chantelle is watching me watch them go.

"You're weird," she says.

I feel too nice to think of a comeback.

When I get home from work at six thirty, my dad is sitting at the kitchen table. There's a plate of barbecued steak, potatoes and carrots in front of him. An identical plate is at my place. In front of an oven, my dad is useless. In front of a barbecue, he's an artist. I sit. I've eaten half my steak and all my carrots before I notice the letter from Red River College at the centre of the table.

"What's that?" I say.

My dad shrugs.

"Came for you," he says.

I get an empty feeling in my chest like my heart slipped out of its spot and it's sliding down my leg into my foot.

"Aren't you going to open it?" my dad asks.

I put down my steak knife and pick up the letter. I rip open the envelope. There's only one piece of paper inside. That could be good or bad. I read. The first words are *Congratulations. You've been accepted into Red River College's Creative Communications Program.* The words that follow don't really register.

I got in!

I put down the letter. I can't hide the giant grin on my face.

"What's it say?" my dad asks.

"I just got into a program at Red River that I really wanted to get in," I say.

"You still on that?" from my dad.

I pick up my steak knife.

"What?"

"You really think you're going to do well in college?" he says. "You work in a gas station. That's all you've ever done. C'mon."

For a moment I entertain the idea of sinking my steak knife deep into his skull through his eye. I decide to put the knife down. I stand and walk over to my dad. I tower over him. I bend down so that my face is an inch away from his ear. He's staring down at his meal.

"Have you ever heard of just being happy for someone, you sad old fuck?" I growl.

I make my way to my room.

"Watch your fucking mouth or you'll be out on the street," my dad shouts.

"Fuck you," I shout back.

In my room, I change into clothes that don't smell like gas station. I put on a ball cap to hide my messy hair. At seven, George is in the driveway. I leave the house without passing my dad. The whole drive into the city, I don't say a word to George. At Jonas's, I don't say a word to anyone. At the bar, I sit by myself and drink. I don't talk to anyone who isn't a bartender, and no one talks to me.

CHAPTER 36

There's a knock at my bedroom door.

"What?" I say.

My dad comes into my room to find me lying on top of my covers in bed, fully clothed. My hands are linked behind my head and I'm staring up at the white ceiling.

"It's two o'clock," he says. "You ever coming outta here?"

"Not really planning on it," I say.

"I read the letter after you left. It said you passed a very extensive entrance process to get into the program you got into, so I guess I should say congratulations," he says.

"Thank you," I say.

"I think my reaction last night was a bad one, and I'd like to apologize. It sounds like you worked really hard to get into college, and I'm happy for you," he says.

"Thank you," I say again.

"I have an offer for you," my dad says. "I will pay the entire cost of your tuition, all of it, on one condition: You spend one day working as a bricklayer labourer. One day. You won't even have to miss work at the gas station. It'll be on a Saturday. You'll get overtime pay. Time and a half. Some of the younger guys do overtime on the weekends if there's a push. You'll work with them. It'll be good for you. You'll see you have options. If you like it, the following Monday, you'll come to work with me. If you decide it's not for you, you go to school in the fall and I'll pay for it. We got a deal?"

I sit up.

"Dad, I've got money," I say. "I can write a cheque and send it off today, and all my tuition would be paid. I can do it on my own."

He motions out the window.

"And how long do you think that piece of shit truck of yours is going to last commuting into the city every day? That thing's three-quarters rust. Wouldn't you much rather keep your money for a new car? Or keep it in the bank so you don't have to work part time at the gas station while you're in school? You'd have more time to do homework and not flunk out," my dad says.

"I'll do just fine," I say.

"Just keep it in mind" my dad says, then makes for the door. "Let me know what you think."

Later that Saturday, Anne and I are enjoying a walk down Corydon. It's just getting dark, but the weather's mild and we're walking in T-shirts. As we pass, Anne glares at the drunken guidos on the patio at Bar Italia who look her up and down, then immediately look away when they meet her eyes firing lasers through them. I smile at this. I tell Anne about my dad's offer. She looks thoughtful for a moment.

"Do it," she says.

"You think so?"

"Yes. Definitely," she says. "CreComm is a pretty intense course. If you can get it paid for and keep all your money for living while you're in school, I say jump on that, man. You won't regret it."

"And what if there's more to this bricklaying shit? Like, if I do a really shitty job, like I know I will, and he's like, 'The wall never got finished, so too bad' or something like that," I say.

"Then you're in the same place you were in before," Anne says. "You'll pay your tuition yourself, you'll work part time at the CountryGas, same as you were planning to."

"And what if I go and I find out I love being a bricklayer labourer?" I ask.

Anne raises her eyebrow at me.

"I'm not religious or anything, but I believe in destiny," she says. "You are destined to write, same as me, same as anyone who uses a pen or a keyboard to earn their pay. That's why we're here. If you go next weekend and decide you're going to build walls until you're sixty, that's fine. That's your choice, but it's not your destiny. You'll lay brick, and in every spare moment you've got, you'll write. It's in your blood, it's in your soul, it's in your eyes. You'll keep writing because it's what you're born to do. And every day you show up to whatever job site you're working at, your soul will die little by little, because you won't be writing for a living like you're meant to. Do you want to do that to yourself? This isn't a question of whether you want to be a bricklayer or a writer. This is a question of whether you want to feed your soul or kill it."

I don't say much for the rest of our walk until we get back to Anne's apartment. I have a lot of thinking to do.

CHAPTER 37

"Don't look," Heidi says.

I look out the window to my right to see Marissa's car pull up. This is where I'm supposed to feel dread. This is where I'm supposed to feel bad about myself. This is where I'm supposed to run and hide in the back office. I turn and smile at Heidi and Erica.

"It's okay," I say, and then I'm outside.

"Hi, Brendan," Marissa says, getting out of her car.

I say hello and ask her how much gas she wants. She asks for a fill. I get it going.

"How's life?" she says.

"Good. Yours?"

"Okay. School's pretty tough."

"I'll bet. You want your windows washed?"

"Um. Sure, I guess."

I set the nozzle so that it pumps on its own, and I grab the squeegee.

"I guess I'll go wait inside," Marissa says.

"Sure thing," I say as I move to the other side of her car.

I'm washing off her taillights when the nozzle clicks off. I put away the squeegee, then top off her car. As I'm walking back into the store, Marissa's walking out. I tip my ball cap to her and tell her to have a nice night.

"Um, thanks," she says.

I'm back in the store. Erica and Heidi have sympathetic eyes. They ask if I'm okay.

"I'm fine," I say. "I'm in a good relationship now with someone far better than her. Honestly, I kinda forgot that she existed."

"Does that mean I have to stop being mean to her?" Heidi asks.

I laugh, and so does she.

CHAPTER 38

"He's so disgusting," Chantelle says.

Oh, what a fucking surprise. She's complaining about someone. I look over at Chantelle. She's standing against the counter, looking at me where I sit on the ladder. She best not be talking about me. No. She's looking at the front page of the newspaper I'm holding. I flip it closed and a picture of Osama bin Laden's face is looking up at me.

"You think he's disgusting?" I ask.

"Uh, yeah!" Chantelle says.

"I think he's attractive."

"Him? That dirty, mass-murdering terrorist?"

"Yeah. He's a good-looking guy."

"You're weird."

"If we're judging him solely on his looks, I have to say he's an eight out of ten, at least."

"He's gross."

"Why, 'cause he has a beard? Jesus had a beard. He looks like Jesus."

"You're fucked. He does not look like Jesus."

"He looks exactly like Jesus."

"Were you there? Did you see him?"

"Did you? I bet Jesus looked exactly like Osama bin Laden," I say.

Four cars pull up to the pumps at the same time.

"You have gas," Chantelle says.

"I sure do. I better go outside," I say.

When I step outside, the driver of the lead car hops out and greets me. The other three cars are at the other three pumps and all the cars have Saskatchewan plates. The driver of the lead car tells me to fill all the cars.

"Bet you've never had cars at all four pumps before, eh?" he says.

It's three in the afternoon. Not the busiest time for gas, but during the morning and after-work rushes, there're cars lined up to get gas.

"Why would we have four pumps if we couldn't have cars at all of them at the same time at different times of the day?" I ask the Saskatchewanian asshole.

He looks like he's trying to solve a very complex riddle, so I ask him why he's visiting Manitoba, and he tells me that his parents live in Oakbank so he packed up the whole family Beverly Hillbillies-style (my words, not his) and came out east for a visit. I listen, uninterested, while he talks shit the entire time I fill his asshole cars about how boring Oakbank is and how there's nothing to do in Winnipeg, either. With a smile, I tell him that maybe he wasn't trying hard enough.

"You gotta see Saskatoon. Now that's a city," he says.

"I'm sure it is," I say.

Later in the shift, I get a much better visit. My friend Kyle walks into the store and says, "Hey," to me. At first I don't recognize him, 'cause I haven't seen him in at least a year and his hair is long and he has a full beard. He looks like a hippie or a Viking or something.

"Holy shit, man," I say. "How's it going?"

"Not bad," he says.

We were good friends in high school before he moved to Alberta to work on oil rigs. His lack of enthusiasm at being home and being in a position to hang out confuses me and makes me even more enthusiastic to compensate. Then again, Kyle was never a really enthusiastic guy.

"You're back," I say.

"I am," he says.

"For how long?"

"For good."

"How come?"

"I made my money. I'm tired of staying in camps. I'm tired of the long hours. I talked to my old boss at the community club. I'm going to go work there again," he says.

"Are you staying with your folks in Cooks Creek?" I ask.

"For now, yeah."

He places a bag of chips on the counter. He pays for them.

"You wanna go to the OBB tonight?" he asks.

"Sure," I say.

"What time you outta here?"

"Six."

"Meet you for seven?"

"Sure thing."

And so at seven o'clock, I'm at the Oakbank Bar like old times, drinking with my buddy Kyle. He drinks double rum and cokes, and I drink Moosehead. Kyle takes in the renovations made in the bar and remarks that it looks less like a shithole in here. I ask him about Alberta and about working on the rigs, and then I wish I hadn't. He talks about his former career very technically, and I can't follow. I can't picture what he's talking about, so I just nod along. Sensing that he's losing me, he tells me a story about a fight he got into in a bar in the middle of Buttfuck Nowhere, Alberta. Some dude got upset with him talking to some girl, and the dude took a few swings at him. Kyle decided he was going to give him a Shawn Michaels-WWF-style superkick but he missed the dude, and there was a window behind the dude and Kyle smashed the shit out of it.

"No way," I say.

After that, Kyle figured it was a good idea to get the fuck out of that bar. He ran bleeding to his truck, drove back to camp drunk and bleeding, and woke up in the morning with his sheets covered in blood. He was okay, though. Just some cuts on his leg.

"Christ," I say.

We trade stories well into the night. I don't have to work until noon tomorrow, so we close down the bar. Kyle offers to drive me home, but considering how many doubles he drank, I decline. I think about telling him to crash at my dad's place, but even after drinking all night, Kyle seems sober, so I let it go. He drives off in his truck and I walk home smoking cigarettes as I go.

I'm so happy Kyle's back. This might be the tow that yanks me out of the rut my social life is in.

CHAPTER 39

Friday, I work all afternoon with Chantelle, counting the minutes until Heidi is set to arrive at four. I'm helping someone behind the counter. Chantelle is watching me. I'm handing the customer his change when she says, "God, you're slow."

I turn to Chantelle. She's trying to smile and trying to pass off what she said like she's just joking around. I'm not buying it.

"Excuse me?" I say.

"What?" she says.

The next customer in line is the blonde lady with the unnatural tan, the breast cancer survivor. She's staring down Chantelle.

"He's not slow," she says. "He's a country boy."

I smile at the customer.

"Thank you," I say. "Matinee Slims?"

"Yes, please."

I hand her her cigarettes. She pays me and leaves.

I turn back to Chantelle. She's not trying to smile anymore.

"You're slow. Really slow," she says.

"Go fuck yourself," I say with a grin.

After work, George stops by my place. I tell him I've got to work Saturday morning for my dad. I tell him about the agreement we've got going, then tell him I won't be going out tonight. George nods, wishes me luck and heads off to the city.

At about eight thirty, I'm sitting in the living room watching D-Day on the History Channel with my dad when the phone rings. I grab the cordless from the coffee table.

"What are you up to tonight?" Kyle asks from the other end.

"Nothing. I'm staying in. I gotta work tomorrow," I say.

"It's Friday night."

"I know, but I gotta be up in the morning."

"Brendan, it's Friday night."

"What do you have in mind?"

"Dinner at the hotel restaurant, and then we'll see from there."

I just ate two hours ago, but it was hotdogs and I feel like I could eat again.

"Okay. I'll leave now," I say.

"Atta boy."

I end the call on the phone and get up from the couch.

"You forget where you need to be in the morning?" my dad asks.

"I'll be there," I say. "I'm just going out for some food. Kyle's back in town."

"I'm going to be banging down your door at five o'clock tomorrow. You better be ready," he says.

"I'll be ready," I say.

I walk to the hotel restaurant that's attached to the Oakbank bar. I leave a trail of cigarette smoke behind me. Kyle is already seated at a table when I arrive. I sit and Carol brings us menus.

"Long time, no see, Brendan," she says. "Where've you been hiding?"

"I'm in the city a lot now," I say.

"I hear you have a girlfriend," she says.

I smile to hide my discomfort.

"Yeah, I do," I say.

Kyle reaches out and shakes Carol's hand.

"My name's Kyle," he says.

And in point zero two seconds, the young waitress has forgotten me.

"Carol," Carol says.

"Kyle does not have a girlfriend," I say.

"No, I do not," he says.

She smiles.

"I'll give you guys a moment to decide," she says, then walks away.

"She's cute," Kyle says, scanning his menu. "You fuck her?"

"Me? No. Nothing like that. Before Anne and I started dating, Carol and I kissed. That's it," I say.

"I can live with that," he says.

"She's a nice girl. Don't fuck around," I say.

"What do you care?"

"'Cause she's nice. Don't fuck her and not call or something."

"Wow. You think highly of me."

"I'm just saying, she's not that kind of girl. Don't be a dick."

"Okay. I'll go against my natural instincts to be a complete dick to this girl."

"You know what I'm saying."

"I think you're saying I'm a dick."

"I just don't know what bad habits you picked up in Alberta."

"I'll be nice. I promise."

Carol returns. I order a bacon cheeseburger and Kyle orders a small pizza.

"After we close up the restaurant, a few of us usually find ourselves in the bar for some after-work drinks. You two are welcome to join us," Carol says, looking only at Kyle.

"Sounds good," he says.

And we do just that. After our meals, we find ourselves in the bar. At around ten thirty, Carol and a couple of others from the restaurant join us. Kyle drinks double after double while talking up Carol, and I carefully monitor my beer intake while keeping mostly to myself, watching the clock. At midnight, I head home.

CHAPTER 40

My alarm goes off at five. My hand darts out lightning fast and shuts it off. I sit up, shake my head and yawn. I stand up and stretch. I had the foresight not to drink too much last night, so I'm not hungover, just tired. I yawn again and get dressed.

I pass my dad's bedroom door on my way to the bathroom. I can hear him snoring. I guess his threat of banging down my door was empty. I take a leak, wash my hands, brush my teeth, splash cold water in my face, towel off and comb my hair. In the kitchen, I make myself toast and coffee. By five thirty, I'm putting on my dad's work boots and grabbing his reflective vest and hard hat. Then I'm out the door and in my shitty truck, heading into the city.

The wall being built is part of an addition to a community club in Transcona. They're building it with big grey cinderblocks. When I get to the site, another labourer and I are told to bring over some tubs of mud, or mortar. A Zoom Boom brings the tubs full of mortar from wherever they're mixing the shit to a spot in the community club parking lot and sets them down, and the other guy and I drag the tubs to the work area. The bricklayers have square, flat pieces of wood set up on blocks, and we shovel out mortar and plop it down on the wood so that they can scoop up mortar with their trowels and lay it on the ground and run their first row, or course, of blocks.

There're pallets full of blocks. We move the blocks from the pallets and set them up in the spaces in between where they've got the wood and mortar set up. This is for easy access for the bricklayers, so they can just turn and grab a block and put it in place. The job of the labourer is essentially making the job of the bricklayer as easy as possible. So far, I've mostly been doing grunt work: dragging, lifting, shoveling, moving. Since I'm a big strong guy, I can handle it. I can do work like this forever. I'm just starting to feel confident when one of the bricklayers starts yelling. His blocks, the blocks I set out for him, are facing the wrong way. One of the other labourers fixes the problem and another one explains to me the proper way of setting them up. I had no idea there was a proper way to stack blocks.

It gets worse from there. When they get to a certain height with the wall, I'm told we have to set up scaffolding for the bricklayers. I've never set up scaffolding in my life, and I'm quite sure it's because of this that the scaffolding is still not properly erected when the bricklayers get as high as they can get with the wall without scaffolding. They hang back and smoke and bitch and yell at us, saying we're costing the boss money, saying that they should be up there already, building the wall. Eventually, we get the scaffolding up and work resumes.

Bricklayers yell and scream and bitch more than any group of people I've ever met. They yell and scream for everything, for more mud, for more blocks, and when you don't deliver fast enough, they bitch. I have no idea what I'm doing so I get yelled at and screamed at and bitched at the most. Other labourers keep having to tell me the proper way of doing things, like how to throw the blocks up onto the scaffolding properly, how to climb up onto the scaffolding properly and how to mix the mortar in the tub to keep it from hardening.

At noon, we stop for lunch. The bricklayers eat at one end of the wall, sitting on blocks, and the labourers eat at the other end of the wall, sitting on blocks. I don't talk to anyone as I eat my corned beef sandwiches, thinking about the new car I can buy after my dad pays my tuition.

The second half of the day goes the same as the first. I fuck up and get yelled at and feel useless and stupid. I wonder why anyone would ever do this. It pays well, but you can survive on less than a bricklayer's wage and not spend the day getting yelled at by gorillas who throw cinderblocks around. I'd sooner spend the rest of my life getting minimum wage to pump gas than ever resort to this, to submit to this kind of abuse. I look around at the other labourers. Some are my age, but most are older. Maybe they have wives and kids to provide for. Maybe this is the hell they must endure to make a good life for their family. Maybe that's what happened to my dad.

That reminds me. I gotta pick up more condoms on my way home.

The afternoon drags but eventually it ends. The other labourers and I clean up as the bricklayers pack up their tools. I thank the guys who helped me out, but otherwise I leave without really saying anything to anyone. I just walk away. I'm never going to see any of these people ever again, so fuck it.

My dad is waiting for me when I get home.

"What the hell happened today?" he demands.

I place his vest and hard hat where I found them this morning and take off his boots.

"What do you mean?" I ask.

"I got a call from Pete," he says.

"Who?"

"Pete. One of the bricklayers you worked with today."

"Oh yeah? What'd he have to say?" I ask.

I'm at the fridge, getting a glass of orange juice. My dad is following me around.

"He said you were a useless tit today," he says.

"That sounds about right," I say.

"I was expecting you to make the effort, not fuck around."

"Who was fucking around? I was making the effort."

"You were there to help out, not slow them down."

"He said I slowed them down?"

"Yeah."

"And whose fault is that, Dad?"

"I'm looking at him."

"No, I'm looking at him."

"This is *my* fault?"

"Yes."

"How the fuck is this my fault?"

"You wanted me there. This was your fucking idea. You were the one who made the arrangements for a guy with no fucking experience to work overtime during a push when speed and experience were necessary to complete the job. You put yourself before the job and the other workers out there today because *you* wanted me there.

This was all about *you* from beginning to end. *You're* to blame," I say.

"I gave you a great opportunity and you fucking blew it," my dad says. "If you think I'm paying for your school, you're fucking dreaming. I don't waste money on losers. You can't even make it as a labourer. What makes you think you'll make it in college?"

I smile.

"I might be a loser, and I might not make it college, but even if I die cold and penniless in a gutter somewhere covered in other people's spit and my own piss, I'll die happy knowing I didn't turn out like you. Now, I'm going to have a shower, I'm going to head into the city and I'm going to hang out with my awesome girlfriend. Have fun spending another night alone watching the History Channel, drinking beer," I say.

I finish my glass of orange juice and place the empty glass in the full sink. Then I'm sidestepping my speechless dad, and I have a shower, I get dressed and I head into the city.

CHAPTER 41

I'm putting on my shoes at Anne's door the next morning. When I straighten up, Anne hugs me, which is strange. She's not a very affectionate person.

"You can just stay," she says. "You don't have to go back there."

I smile.

"He's been threatening to kick me out since I turned sixteen," I say. "I might go home to changed locks."

"Was it that bad?"

"It wasn't good."

"Well, if he kicks you out, you come right back here. You're always welcome here," Anne says.

"Yeah? You want a roommate?" I ask.

"Fuck yes," she says. "Have my rent split in half? Fuck yes."

We laugh and we kiss, and I leave. The drive back to Oakbank is the longest I've ever driven. My mind reels, exploring all the possible scenarios, all the possible things he could say to me when I get home, all the possible things I might say. This could be ugly, but more than likely he'll say nothing to me, not for days, and all that was said last night will sink down below the surface only to rise up worse than before the next time we have it out. This is what we do. This is functioning dysfunction.

I'm not expecting my dad to surprise me, but that's what he does. I walk into the house, into the kitchen to see that it's clean. The sink is empty of dirty dishes and the dishwasher is going. There're pots and pans in the dryer rack. The counter is wiped clean and the floor is mopped and smells of Mr. Clean. There's another smell. Bacon. There's a plateful sitting on the oven. I want to walk over and eat it all, but I don't. My dad is sitting at the table with a plate of eggs, bacon and toast. He's drinking coffee.

"Morning," he says.

"Morning," I say.

"There's lots of bacon. I didn't make you eggs 'cause I didn't know when you'd be home. Coffee's fresh," my dad says.

I pour myself a cup, grab two pieces of bacon and sit at the table. I eat one full piece of bacon before I speak.

"Last night I said some things I didn't mean. I'm sorry," I say.

My dad waves a dismissive hand.

"No. You meant it, and I deserved it," he says.

He takes a sip of coffee. I have no idea what to say, what to do.

"So ... what's up?" I finally manage.

My dad lets out a long, loud sigh.

"After you left last night, I thought about what you said. I poured myself a Scotch and thought about it. Then I had another Scotch, and another. And it was about then, after that third Scotch, that I remembered something. It came clear to me. Everything became clear to me," he says.

I'm chewing on a mouthful of bacon. I've never been so anxious in my life. Is he going to hug me? Is he going to toss me out? Is he going to kill me? What?

"What became clear to you?" I ask.

"It was a promise I made twenty years ago, when you were a baby in the hospital in the arms of your shit-scared dad. I made a promise ... to you or to God or to myself, I don't know. But I made it. It meant something. And as you grew up, I forgot about that promise. But I remembered it last night. It came to me like a vision. Like a goddamn epiphany," my dad says.

I finish my bacon and take a sip of coffee.

"What did you remember?"

My dad smiles awkwardly at me.

"You got a cigarette on you?" he asks.

I'm digging frantically into my jeans pocket for my pack. I take out a smoke and hand it to him. I light it for him. He drags deep and lets out powerful lungfuls of smoke. He looks quite satisfied for a moment, then holds the cigarette out in front of him.

"It's been ten years since I had one of these," he says.

"I know, Dad," I say. "What did you remember?"

My dad takes another drag.

"I promised that I was going to work hard, as hard as I could, no matter what, so that my little boy would grow into a man different from me, a man who could hold the world in his hand and do anything and be anyone he wanted to be. That was the promise I made when I first held you. I worked hard to give you a good life, to give you a leg up, so you could be better than me. I worked hard, and it cost me a marriage, but I was working towards something," he says.

He ashes his cigarette on the plate beside him on the table. The ashes cling to the remaining yolk left from his eggs.

"I wanted you to have all the advantages that I never had. When I was growing up, a man made a living using his strength, not his brain. So that's what I did. And now you're all grown, smart like your mom, and you're going to go to college, and I'm trying my damnedest to make you exactly like me. I'm trying to make you a broken-down old man. I worked so hard so you wouldn't have to be like me, and now I'm trying to throw that away and turn you into a fucking bricklayer. What fucking sense does that make?" my dad says.

I laugh and thankfully he does too. It was either laugh or cry.

"I think we fight sometimes 'cause we're so different," I say, the words finding their way past the lump in my throat.

He shakes his head.

"We're not that different," he says. "I enjoyed writing when I was in school. I really did. I'd come home from school and sit and do my homework and write my essays, and your grandmother would come along and say, 'What're you wasting your time with that for? That's lazy work. Go do your chores outside.' And I did."

My dad's cigarette is done. It's nothing but filter. He snuffs it out in the egg yolk on his plate.

"The big difference between you and me is that I did what people expected of me and you did whatever the fuck made you happy. And I couldn't be prouder," he says.

I take a sip of coffee to dislodge the lump in my throat.

"Thanks, Dad," I say.

He gets up from his chair.

"Needless to say, I'll be paying for your school like I said I would. Make sure you eat the rest of the bacon," he says. "I'm going to have a nap. I got up pretty early to clean the kitchen, and I'm still a little hungover from all the Scotch."

My dad retires to his room. I get up and go outside and sit on the back step and light a cigarette of my own.

What the fuck just happened? That was completely out of left field. He doesn't want me to be like him? He likes writing? He's proud of me? What was in that Scotch last night? Am I still at Anne's? Am I dreaming? Am I dead? Did I veer off the highway on the way home and hit a hydro pole? Is this heaven?

I pinch myself.

Nope. Still alive. Not dreaming.

I decide to be cautious. This could be a momentary lapse in the status quo. Our natural state is to be at odds with each other. When he wakes from his nap, he could be back to his old self. People don't just change overnight, especially not old racist construction workers.

My dad can say whatever the fuck he wants. Until he starts walking the walk, nothing has changed for me. He'll still be the same unpleasant old fuck who drove away my mom.

CHAPTER 42

Mary's rusted-out van pulls up to the pumps and I head outside. She asks me for a fill, but this time she stays in her vehicle. When the fill is done, she hands me cash and I run in to get her change. I run back out with a handful of small bills and coins. I hand it to Mary through her open driver's side window.

"Have you seen *Left Behind* yet?" she asks me.

"No. Not yet."

"Soon?"

I just want her to leave.

"Yeah. Sure."

"Would you like a pamphlet?" Mary asks.

"Okay," I say and take the pamphlet she hands me

without looking at it.

Mary says goodbye and I say goodbye and she drives off. I don't look at the pamphlet until I'm back in the store, behind the counter. The title reads *Jesus, Abstinence and AIDS*.

"What the fuck?" I say.

Heidi is beside me in an instant. I show her my new literature and we have a laugh.

After work, after I make dinner for my dad and myself, I head into the city to Jonas's place. Lost Astronaut is practising in the basement. They practise every weekday evening, presumably in an effort to drive Jonas's mother insane. The band is their part-time job. They take it very seriously. They may not play a lot of shows, but they're as refined and polished as a garage band (or basement band) gets. They're just hard rock enough to attract dudes, and they're just hair metal enough to attract women. They're classic rock enough to appeal to the old folks, and they're modern rock enough to appeal to the kids. Marketed properly, they could be the next big Canadian rock band.

I sit on the couch and watch and listen to my friends play. Right now, they're just a bunch of buddies having fun. I forget about the drugs and the underage girls and the out-of-control partying, and I tap my foot along to George's bass drum.

CHAPTER 43

I'm filling a car. The asshole driver of the car is sitting inside. The nozzle clicks off at $38.43. I pull the nozzle out a tiny bit and continue pumping slowly. The nozzle clicks off at $38.87. Very slowly, I top the car off to an even thirty-nine dollars.

The asshole customer has her head out the window.

"What was that sound?" she demands.

"What sound?" I ask, hanging up the nozzle.

"That clicking sound?" she says.

"Oh. That's just the nozzle clicking off. It does that to tell me the tank is full," I say.

"Does it damage my car?" she asks.

"Huh? No."

"Are you sure?"

"The part that makes the clicking sound is in the handle of the nozzle. It doesn't touch your car. It's not hurting your car," I say.

"Well, my husband's a mechanic. I'm going to have him look at my car, and if it's damaged, I'll be back to talk to your manager," she says.

It's amazing that people can get indignant about things they have no idea about.

I smile.

"I assure you, your car is fine," I say.

"We'll see," she says.

She gives me two twenties, I go inside and get her a dollar change, I give it to her and she's on her way.

It's Friday, so shortly after work I find myself at Jonas's. I'm playing video games with George when Davis walks up and blocks the TV. He tells me that Marc isn't coming out with us tonight 'cause he's going to check out some band or something. Davis asks me to come with him to pick up drugs from JT. Reluctantly, I agree to go.

In Davis's car, I notice we're going a different way.

"I thought we're picking up from JT?" I say.

"We are," Davis says. "He's renting a house with his girlfriend near Park Circle now. You'll see."

After navigating the dark streets of Transcona for a little while, we pull up in front of a house that looks like it hasn't seen proper maintenance in years. We go to the side door and JT's girlfriend lets us in. She looks thinner than the last time I saw her. Not I've-been-doing-exercise-tapes thinner. She looks I've-been-doing-coke-for-months-straight thinner.

We're told JT's in the basement, so we head down carpeted stairs into an unfinished basement with a concrete floor, exposed wooden studs and exposed electrical work. JT is sitting in the centre of the room on a lawn chair with another man who's also sitting on a lawn chair. Between them is a table that is actually a wooden spool turned on its side. On top of the spool are a wide variety of drugs and drug paraphernalia. JT has his pipe and he's smoking little white balls that I hope aren't crack.

I'm grinding my teeth. I don't like this place.

JT sees us and waves us over.

"What you guys want?" he asks Davis.

"Same as always," Davis says.

The other man sitting, the man I don't know, speaks up.

"I have to go, JT," he says.

He's fucked out of his tree. JT forgets Davis and I are here.

"Shut your fucking mouth, Dobbs. You ain't going nowhere," JT says.

"I have to go, JT," Dobbs says again. "My babies. My wife and my babies. I gotta go back to them. I gotta go, JT."

JT points a finger across the table.

"Shut your fucking mouth, Dobbs," he says. "You ain't leaving yet. You're gonna sit here all night if I say so. Shut your mouth."

JT goes back to dealing with Davis. I'm watching Dobbs. He's squirming and writhing in his lawn chair, like a kid at the dinner table who doesn't want to eat. He looks like he's near tears. What the fuck is going on here?

Davis and JT are trading drugs for money when Dobbs stands. JT quickly pockets the money and turns his attention back to Dobbs.

"Sit the fuck back down, faggot," he barks. "You'll leave when I let you leave."

"I have to go home to my babies," Dobbs blubbers.

This exchange continues as Davis and I climb the stairs and leave the shithole house the same way we came in. Back in the car, I turn to Davis.

"Does JT have a gun?" I ask.

"Huh? How should I know?" Davis says.

"You do business with him routinely," I say. "I think I'd like to know whether the person I do business with on a regular basis has a fucking Glock 9 hidden down the ass of his pants."

"He doesn't have a gun."

"No?"

"No."

"You know this for sure?"

"I've never seen him with a gun."

"Doesn't mean he doesn't have one."

"Marc knows him from high school. He's cool," Davis says.

"No, man, he's the opposite of cool. He's fucking tweaked out. He's a coke dealer, which means for fucking sure he's got a gun. He's probably getting coke from the Hells Angels, from people we want nothing to do with. This is fucked up, man, and it's fucked up that you think this is cool and not fucked up at all," I say.

Davis laughs.

"You always do this," he says.

"Do what? I don't think I've ever been in this situation before," I say.

"You blow things out of proportion," Davis says. "Anytime you get uncomfortable with something, you pick it apart and dissect it and blow it up like you're doing now. All we did is pick up some drugs and you're talking about guns and the fucking Hells Angels. Just settle down. Be cool. Everything's fine."

"Sorry for digging only slightly deeper into the situation," I say.

"Just be cool, man. Everything's fine," Davis says again.

That night I spend the entire time wishing I were somewhere else. I decide that I'm no longer going to let George pick me up. From now on I'll always have my truck with me. In case I need an escape.

CHAPTER 44

"I think I need new friends," I tell Anne.

We're sitting on her couch. She's resting against my side, her head on my shoulder. We're watching a movie.

"So get new friends," she says.

"Should I take out an ad in the paper?" I ask. "How do you make new friends as an adult?"

"I wouldn't worry too much about it," Anne says. "You're just at a shitty age where you realize your high school friends aren't going to be your lifelong friends. People drift apart. It's natural. It happens. There's one person that I still keep in touch with from high school, and we only talk on the phone maybe once a month. All my friends I have now are from CreComm."

"Why is that?" I ask.

Anne sits up.

"It's a dating service. Sort of. It operates the same way. You take five hundred applicants and whittle that number down to seventy-five people who all love writing, who all have a lot in common. Then you put them all in the same course and you allow them to get to know each other through constant contact and group projects. The course is really intense so everyone has this strong bond. It's a dating service for friends. Essentially," Anne says.

"You think that will happen with me when I go?" I ask.

"Most definitely," she says. "Just don't forget about me when you're having fun with your new best friends."

I make a face at her.

"How could I forget about you? Every good thing I have in my life right now I have because of you," I say.

"Shut up."

"It's true. If not for you, I wouldn't be going back to school, and if not for going back to school, me and my dad wouldn't have had the argument we did and things wouldn't be good between us for the first time in years, so thank you," I say.

"You would have made all that stuff happen yourself eventually," Anne says.

"No, you're a sorceress woman who has complete control over my life and my decisions," I say.

"Like a witch?"

"Exactly like a witch."

"Excellent. I'm finally a witch."

Some kissing happens after this. So as not to gross you out, I won't tell you about it.

After the kissing, I say, "Do you want to meet my dad?"

"Sure, why not?" Anne says.

Okay. So then it's settled.

Anne gets up and ejects the movie from her DVD player. With the TV off DVD mode, it shows CNN. George Bush's giant head is on the screen. Anne gives her TV the finger.

"Not a fan?" I say, laughing.

"I hate that asshole," she says.

"Maybe he won't find bin Laden and the Americans will impeach him," I say.

"They won't find bin Laden," Anne says.

"No?"

"No. They need bin Laden," she says. "Bush needs his little boogeyman. That's his blank cheque. Anytime he wants something passed, he'll bring up bin Laden and terrorism and domestic security. He'll get shit like the Patriot Act passed and everyone will think it's a tool to fight terror, but it's not. It's a tool to extend his empire, both at home and abroad. Afghanistan is just the beginning. They're going to spread out all over the Middle East, like they spread out into Laos and Cambodia during the Vietnam War. They'll install puppet governments that'll let them set up bases and sell us cheap oil, and they'll sit back and watch the money roll in. This isn't a war on terror. This is a jihad. It's a holy war. We've got Christian fundamentalists joining the army to kill Islamic fundamentalists halfway around the world. It's so wrong."

I'm silent a moment.

"Anne, how do you reconcile your anarchism with the fact that you work for an advertising company?" I ask.

"I have no problem taking money from advertisers so that I can have a roof over my head and food on my table. They own my writing; they don't own me. If they're willing to give me money to write for them, great, but that's as far as it goes. Then, in my spare time, I do this," she says. Then she walks into her bedroom.

She comes out with a photo album and sits next to me and opens it.

"These are pictures from the anti-war rallies I've been to. There usually aren't a lot of us, but we're persistent. We're out there. We're doing something. People talk and talk and talk about how shitty things are, but they don't do anything. We're out in the streets where everyone can see. We're fighting, y'know? When the revolution comes, and it's coming, it won't be the hippies and the potheads who effect change. It'll be people like me with jobs who can change things from the inside. We're the viruses in the system. We're the cancer cells in the host body. You see what I'm saying?" Anne asks.

I nod. "I see."

CHAPTER 45

I'm in my room, getting dressed after my after-work shower. The doorbell rings and I can hear my dad talking to someone. After only half a minute, I hear him say, "Not interested." Then the door closes. Fully dressed, I come out of my room.

"What was all that about?" I ask.

My dad is sitting on the couch again.

"Religious nut," he says.

He motions to the table by the front door. I walk over to it. On it sits a pamphlet. The title reads *Jesus, God and You*.

"Fuck off," I say. I go to the window in time to see Mary walking away from the house, down the sidewalk. "What the fuck?"

"Fucking Jesus freak," my dad says.

I turn to him.

"You still want to do this tonight?" I ask him.

"Of course," he says.

"I can call Anne, and we can do this another time," I say.

"Tonight's fine," my dad says. "You go get your little lady and I'll fire up the barbecue. Your lady —"

"Anne."

"— she's not one of them vegetarians, is she?"

"No, she's not."

"Good, 'cause I'm making my special hamburgers. The ones with the diced onions inside," he says.

"Sounds good," I say. I'm back at the door putting my shoes on. "I'll be back in an hour or so."

I get into my shitty little truck and I drive into the city. I park outside Anne's building and I buzz her apartment. Anne comes down in a plain black T-shirt and black jeans. She's dressed as she always dresses, and I like that. She's not trying to impress anyone. She's just being herself.

Less than an hour after I left my dad's place, I'm back. Anne and I can smell burgers in the backyard, and there we find my dad grilling. My dad is full of surprises lately. He's nothing but warm and inviting to Anne. I keep expecting him to be his insulting, curmudgeonly self, but early in the visit I find I'm able to put my guard down. He's not putting on an act with Anne. He's opening up a genuine part of himself, the friendly side, the side I never see. He's almost charming, and for the first time I understand how an Irish bricklayer from Manitoba could woo an Italian woman from Toronto. For the first time, I see what my mother must have seen in him years ago.

"So, do you exaggerate often?" Anne asks me, sitting next to me in my truck as I drive her home.

"What do you mean?" I ask.

"Your dad isn't half the monster you made him out to be," she says.

"I'm shocked. He was a teddy bear tonight. Did you have a good time?" I ask.

"I did," Anne says. "You said before that you owe me, Brendan. You said that everything good in your life right now is because of me. I think you've got it wrong. You don't owe me anything. I owe you. And it's not just the sleep thing, although I have only you to thank for that. I feel like I'm a better person when I'm with you. And it could be because I'm sleeping again and I don't hate life anymore, but you met me when I wasn't sleeping, when I did hate life. You met me at my worst and you still saw something in me, and you helped make me the person I am now. I'm happy now and I have you to thank for that happiness."

I turn and smile at Anne, then return my attention to the highway.

"I'd kiss you, but I think that might land us in the ditch," I say.

Anne laughs.

"Maybe just keep your eyes on the road."

CHAPTER 46

Maybe I do exaggerate things. Maybe I do blow things out of proportion. Maybe I see only the bad and never the good. Maybe Davis is right. Maybe I just need to be cool.

I take my own truck to Jonas's place on Friday simply as a precaution. If things go horribly wrong, I have a way out. But I'm not going to expect things to go horribly wrong. I'm going to be fun tonight. I'm going to be my best self. I'm going to interact and create memories. I'm young and my life is going great. No sense in being a stick in the mud. I'm going to be cool.

It's a disaster.

I drink too much at the bar. Then when we get back to Jonas's, I'm sitting at the kitchen table, already spinning a little. Marc rolls a joint, and in the spirit of being cool and being fun, I take some hits. Within minutes of smoking up, I feel like I'm going to throw up. The house is full of people. I don't want to occupy the main bathroom forever, so I go to Jonas's mom's room, to her en suite bathroom. I kneel at the toilet and throw up. When I'm done throwing up, I turn out the light and pass out.

I come to an indeterminate amount of time later. Jonas's mom's room is just down the hall from the kitchen, where I can hear the guys talking.

"Where the fuck is Brendan?" Marc asks.

"Who cares? Do you want him here?" Jonas asks.

"That guy's a fucking buzzkill, man," Davis says.

That's the part of their conversation that pertains to me. They talk about other shit after that. It's nice to know how I'm spoken of when I'm not around.

I pass back out only to be woken up violently another indeterminate amount of time later when Jonas throws on the light in the en suite.

"What the fuck are you doing in my mom's room?" he yells.

I get up and walk past him out of the bathroom, out of his mom's room, but all the walking makes my head spin and I know I'm going to throw up again. I feel it crawling up my throat. I try the doorknob for the main bathroom but it's locked, so I do the only thing I can think to do under the circumstances. I go to the kitchen sink and throw up.

I can hear the guys yelling in disgust behind me. There's nothing much I can do. I just keep throwing up. Something flies through the air and crashes into the wall just above my head. It comes to rest on the counter in view. It's a box of Rice-A-Roni. Another box hits the drapes on the little window behind the sink. A third box hits me dead centre in the back. The corner hits me. It hurts like a motherfucker.

They're throwing shit at me.

They laugh as I finish puking and I run the water to wash away my puke. I turn around. Marc, Jonas and Davis are standing by the open pantry at the other end of the kitchen. Marc and Jonas continue laughing and move down the hall out of sight, but Davis stays where he is, looking at me like I'm the lowest piece of shit.

My legs are steady. My head is no longer spinning. Rage has drained the effects of drugs and alcohol from my body. I beeline straight to Davis, I shove my forearm up under his chin into his throat and I slam him into the wall.

"I'm throwing up, so you throw shit at me? Is that what friends do?" I shout.

Marc and Jonas are beside me in an instant.

"Let him go, Brendan," Marc says.

"Fuck you," I shout at Marc. Then I shout at Davis, "You're pretty tough when I'm bent over throwing up. You're not so tough now."

"Brendan, you gotta leave. I don't want you in my house," Jonas says.

I release Davis.

"What the fuck makes you think I want to stay here?" I say. "You guys are fucked."

Then I'm putting my shoes on and I'm gone. I drive drunk for the first time since I was arrested for drinking and driving. The whole way home, I treat every other car as if it's a cop.

CHAPTER 47

The next day, I have no intention of leaving my room. At three in the afternoon, my dad knocks on the door and opens it to find me lying out on my covers wearing the same clothes as last night.

"You getting up, kid?" he asks.

"Yeah."

"It smells like a brewery in here."

"Yeah."

"You drive home last night?"

"Yeah."

"You drank and drove?"

"Yeah."

"Why the fuck did you do that?"

"I got kicked out of Jonas's place."

"How come?"

"I got drunk and threw up, and they started throwing shit at me, so I slammed Davis into a wall," I say.

My dad is silent a moment.

"Fucking A. Don't take no shit," he says, then leaves.

I lie there without moving for another half hour or so. Then I shower and wash the lingering disgusting off me. Feeling only slightly better, I dress and head into the living room. My dad is at the front door talking to someone.

"What part of 'not interested' don't you understand?" I hear him say.

I walk up beside him and open the door wide. Standing on the front porch, holding her pamphlets, is Mary. Her eyes get wide when she sees me.

"Hi, Brendan," she says. "I was just talking to your dad about —"

"You know this woman?" my dad asks.

"Mary, what are you doing here?" I ask.

She smiles.

"Just spreading the word of the Lord," she says.

"Mary, we're atheists," I say, motioning to my dad and myself.

"Then I came to the right place," she says.

"No, you didn't. Don't come back here again," I say.

"I'll be praying for you both," Mary says, stepping down from the porch.

"Or you can do nothing. Same thing," I say, and I close the door.

"Who was that fucking loon?" my dad asks as I sit on the couch.

"She comes to the gas station handing out pamphlets," I say. "She's a Jesus freak."

"You said it," he says.

After a few hours of hanging out with my dad, I drive into the city to hang out with Anne. I sit on her couch, and she goes to her entertainment unit.

"What do you want to watch, *A Beautiful Mind* or *Donnie Darko?*" she asks.

I make a displeased sound.

"What?" she says.

"Do you really want to sit and watch a movie tonight? That's all we ever do lately," I say.

"What do you want to do?" she asks.

"Something. Anything," I say.

"Are you hungry?"

"I could eat."

"You want to go for dinner?"

"That sounds good."

"You ever been to Krystina's? Krystina's on Corydon?"

"No. Is it good?"

"It's really good. Let's go."

And we do. We're seated at our table for no more than a minute before Anne hits me with, "So, what's up your ass today?"

I consider saying nothing.

"I had a falling out with my friends last night," I say. Then I tell her the story.

"That sucks," Anne says. "Your friends sound like douchebags."

"They can be."

"So why are you upset? Now you don't have to deal with them anymore."

"They were my only friends."

"That can't be true."

"They were my oldest friends."

"Sounds like it's time to make some new, better friends."

"Yeah."

"And remember, you've still got me."

Anne reaches across the table and touches my hand, and she gives me one of her rare warm smiles. My attention is diverted from her smile to a man walking over to our table from a crowded corner of the restaurant. He, too, has a smile on his face, but it looks like it's hurting him to wear it. He stops at our table and stands smiling his weird smile at me.

"Yes?" I say.

He turns to Anne, and Anne drops her gaze to the table.

"Hi, Anne," the man says.

She looks out the window to her left, away from him. The man looks back to me.

"Is this the guy?" he says, pointing.

Anne says nothing. The man bends down to me a bit.

"She's your mess now. Have fun cleaning her up," he says. Then he does an about-face turn and leaves the restaurant.

Anne and I don't speak the entire meal except to order from our waiter. Once we're back at her apartment, I ask the question that's been burning in my mind all night.

"Anne, who was that guy?"

She has her back to me, hanging her hoodie on a chair back. She's very still. She turns.

"That was my ex. Richard," she says.

"Why'd he ask, 'Is this the guy?'?"

"Richard and I weren't exactly done yet when I met you."

"How not done were you?"

"We were engaged."

It takes me a moment to process this.

"When did you two get engaged?" I ask.

"About a year before I met you. That's when the insomnia started."

"When did you break off the engagement?"

"A few weeks after we first had sex."

"You cheated on him with me?"

"Yes."

I still have my shoes on. I'm standing next to the door. I reach for the knob. Anne is over to me in an instant.

"I didn't love him, Brendan. He wanted to marry me, and I didn't love him. I couldn't sleep. I was trapped. Then I met you and you were everything he wasn't and I fell in love with you. I slept when I was with you. I knew in my heart that you were the one I should be with. I changed everything to be with you, and I'm glad 'cause everything is better with you. Do you understand me? Everything is better with you. Please don't go," she says.

"If you really wanted to be with me, you would have done this right," I say. "Goodbye."

And I leave.

CHAPTER 48

I don't want to talk about it.

CHAPTER 49

I go outside to the car that pulled up to the pumps. The driver asks for twenty dollars and hands me a twenty. After I get it going, the asshole customer sticks his head out of his window.

"Hey there, chief," he says. "How often do you test for water in the tanks?"

"There's no water in the tanks," I say without looking at him.

"Are you sure? How do you know for sure?" he says.

"We test for water once a month. There's no water."

"Once a month isn't very often."

"It's often enough."

"It's just that I got gas here last week and my car was running funny after."

"Maybe there's something wrong with your car."

"Yeah, like maybe I got gas with water in it."

The numbers on the pump flip over to twenty dollars, and I pull the nozzle out of the man's car and hang it up. I walk over to his window.

"Sir, the entire town gets gas here. Only you have complained about there being something wrong with the gas. Now, is it possible that there was water in our tanks and somehow that water found its way into your gas tank exclusively, or is it more likely that you're having problems with your shitty, rusted-out Honda Accord and you want my boss to pay for the repairs?" I say.

The man rolls up his window and drives away.

"Fucking asshole," I say and go inside.

Erica is serving Marissa. She's buying cigarettes. When she gets her change, she turns to me, smiles and says, "Hi, Brendan."

And I see red. I cannot hold my tongue.

"Why are you here, Marissa?" I ask.

"I needed smokes," she says.

"Why do you continue to come here?" I ask.

Nothing.

I point at Erica and at Heidi.

"I don't want you here. She doesn't want you here. She doesn't want you here. Why don't you find another gas station? There're millions of them," I say.

"This is the closest one to my house," Marissa says.

"Well, I work here and I don't want you here, so find a new one," I say.

She's quiet a moment, standing between the cash counter and the door.

"You hate me, don't you, Brendan?" she says.

I smile.

"No, I don't hate you, Marissa. I *fucking* hate you. Now fuck off," I say.

And she does. She puts her pack of cigarettes in her purse and slowly leaves. If I still had a heart, I'd feel bad, but I don't so I don't.

"Brendan, can I see you in my office, please?" Jane speaks up from the doorway leading to the back of the store.

Oh shit. Busted. I didn't see her standing there. I leave the front and follow Jane into her little office. She doesn't look too happy with me.

"What the hell was that, Brendan?" she asks.

"I'm sorry," I say. "I have some history with that girl."

"No, you don't. Not here. Not while you're working. When you're working and she comes in, she's just another customer. You give her what she wants and you smile and say, 'Have a nice day.' You leave your personal baggage at home when you come work for me," Jane says.

"I know. I'm sorry," I say.

"I can't have you up there swearing at customers, Brendan," she says.

"It won't happen again," I say.

"If you were anyone else, you'd be fired. But you've been a really good worker and this is the first time I've had to talk to you in what ... two years?" she asks.

"About that," I say.

Jane smiles.

"Go finish your shift," she says. "Just don't swear at the customers anymore."

I smile and thank my boss. Then I head back to work.

CHAPTER 50

It's Friday after work and I'm lying over my covers in bed wearing my smelly work clothes. I'm listening to Elliott Smith on my stereo. *Either/Or*. It's the saddest one. The punk CDs Anne got me for Christmas are in the little garbage can in the corner of my room.

The phone rings. I hear my dad answer it, and then I hear his footsteps getting louder as they approach my door. He opens it, hands me the phone and leaves.

It's Heidi.

"How's it going, Brendan?" she asks.

"Good."

"You didn't seem good this week. You seemed kinda depressed."

"Nah. I'm okay."

"Is that Elliott Smith you're listening to?"

"Um, yeah."

"I just thought I'd call to make sure you're okay. I've known people who've been really depressed and they go home and do something bad," Heidi says.

"Oh God," I say. "You think I'm suicidal?"

"Well ..."

"I'm fine, Heidi," I say. "I'm not going to kill myself. Thanks for your concern. You're a great person, and I'll see you at work on Monday."

"You're sure you're fine?"

"Yes. Goodbye," I say and hit end on the cordless phone.

Suddenly, I don't want to listen to Elliott Smith anymore. I dig my Alkaline Trio CD out of the trash and put it on. I lie back down on my bed. Not five minutes since he last visited my room, my dad is back.

"Your friend is here," he says.

I go outside to see George's truck parked in the driveway. George is standing by the driver's side door.

"Hey," he says when I walk up.

"Hey," I say.

"Shit got pretty crazy last weekend," he says.

"You can say that," I say.

"You coming with me tonight?" he asks.

"No fucking way," I say.

"The guys feel bad about how everything went down," he says.

"Their true colours came out. I don't think I want to waste my time with them anymore. I'm done," I say.

"You know I wasn't a part of that, right?"

"Yeah."

"I was in the bathroom throwing up, too."

"Oh."

"And if I saw you throwing up, my first instinct wouldn't be to throw shit at you."

"Thanks, man. I just think I need a break, y'know?" I say.

"From what?" George asks.

"From all of you," I say.

George nods.

"Fair enough," he says.

We don't say much after that. George gets into his truck and leaves, and I head back inside. After I take a shower and change into clean clothes, the cordless phone starts ringing on my bed. I answer it.

It's Kyle.

"Hey, man," he says. "What're your plans for tonight?"

"Got none," I say.

"You wanna hang out?" he asks.

If I were still listening to Elliott Smith, I would say no. Now that I'm listening to something a little more upbeat, I say, "Sure."

"Cool," Kyle says. "Meet me at the Oak. I got a hotel room at the Club Regent Casino. We'll go there after."

"Why?"

"Why what?"

"Why'd you get a hotel room?"

"So we can get crazy drunk and have somewhere to crash in the city," he says.

"Oh. Cool."

"See ya in a bit."

"Yeah. See ya."

Forty-five minutes later, I'm sitting at a table in the Oak with Kyle.

"So," he says, "what happened with Davis and those guys last weekend?"

I tell him the story.

"Is that what happened?" he says. "I ran into Davis this week and he said you had a full-on mental breakdown. He said you were puking everywhere and destroying everything and you assaulted him. He said you were like a drunken Godzilla."

I laugh.

"Is that right?"

"Yeah. I figured it was bullshit. It didn't really sound

like you, to get all pissed off for no reason," Kyle says.

"No. I had a reason," I say.

I want the topic of our conversation to change.

"Where's Carol tonight?" I ask.

"How should I know?" he says.

"Aren't you two together?"

"No."

"Oh. You guys seemed pretty chummy at the OBB that time."

"Nah. It didn't go much further than that. You freaked me out with all that 'She's a nice girl, treat her right' talk," Kyle says.

"Okay," I say.

"I don't want a nice girl, Brendan," he says. "I want a girl that'll ruin my life."

"I guess we differ on that," I say.

"I just spent two of my prime years working with a bunch of guys in Alberta. Now that I'm back in civilization, I'm not going to find some nice girl and settle down and get married and have a bunch of stupid kids. I'm going to make up for lost time," he says.

"Have fun," I say.

Kyle is looking past me, over my shoulder towards the bar.

"Stay here," he says. "There's a girl over there that looks like she eats dicks for breakfast."

He gets up from the table and fucks off, leaving me alone to drink my beer. I've been sitting for ten minutes when two women stop at my table.

"Brendan?" one of them says.

I look up and smile. I recognize the woman as a girl I used to know in junior high. Her name is Janelle. She was the neighbour of one of the guys I first played in a band with back in grade eight. She'd come and hang out with us while we practised. She was a good shit. Her friend I don't recognize. To be honest, her friend looks like, and is dressed like, she just came from a porn shoot.

The two of them sit with me for a while, and Janelle and I catch up. Kyle is still off doing whatever the hell he's doing. I mention to Janelle that we have a hotel room for after the bar. I tell her that she and her friend should come and hang out with us after. They seem excited about this and they excuse themselves to go get new drinks.

And suddenly I feel bad. Anne and I have been done for a week, and now I'm some creepy guy who invites women back to hotel rooms after the bar? What the fuck?

No. This is normal. This is what young guys do. They go to bars, they pick up girls and they take them to a secondary location for sex. This is what they do, all over the city, all over the country, all over the world. This is normal.

Then why doesn't it feel normal to me?

I don't see Kyle again for the rest of the night. I don't see Janelle or her friend either. Nor do I see the Lost Astronaut guys, which is good. I was concerned I was going to run into them. At two in the morning, the house lights come on while couples dance their last dance of the night. I head outside into the parking lot.

"Brendan!"

Janelle and her friend rush up to me.

"Do you and your friend still have that hotel room?" she asks me.

"Uh, yeah. I'm heading there now," I say.

"Can we still come?" she asks.

"If you guys want."

"Yeah. We'll be there in a little bit."

"Okay," I say and give them the room number.

We part ways and I walk down Regent Avenue to the casino. I walk into the hotel and I go up three floors in the elevator and find Kyle's room. I knock on the door.

After a moment, the door opens a crack. The chain is on and the lights in the room are off. From the light in the hallway I can see that Kyle is wearing only boxers.

"You going to let me in?" I ask.

"Can you go somewhere for a little while?" he asks.

"It's two thirty in the morning," I say. "Where am I going to go?"

Kyle makes a face.

"I've got a call girl in here and I've still got another twenty minutes with her," he says.

It takes me a moment to process this.

"Kyle, I've got two real girls coming to this room any time now, and you've got a fucking call girl in there?" I say.

"You've got girls coming here?" he says.

"Yes. Where have you been all night?" I say.

Kyle takes the chain off the door and opens it.

"Go into the bathroom. When the girls get here, take them into the bathroom with you. I won't be long," he says.

Fuck my life. Seriously.

I go into the bathroom. I put the seat down on the toilet and I sit, smoking compulsively, ashing in the tub. I wait, listening for a knock at the door. It doesn't come. After about fifteen minutes and three cigarettes, I can hear talking at the door. Kyle is seeing the call girl out. More than anything, I want to see what she looks like. I'm picturing big hair and lots of makeup, but when I open the bathroom door I see that the woman leaving looks like a normal woman, no different from Janelle or Erica or any of the other women in my life.

Or Anne.

Seeing the non-whorish whore really bums me out. What causes an otherwise normal woman to go to a hotel in the middle of the night to fuck some dude for money?

Kyle closes the door.

"That was close, huh?" he says. "When are your girls coming?"

I still have my shoes on. I leave, too.

I'm walking out of the hotel as Janelle and her friend are coming in.

"Brendan? Where are you going?" Janelle asks.

"I'm going to go sleep in my truck."

CHAPTER 51

After the hooker incident, I go into hermit mode. When I'm not at work, I'm at home in my room listening to sad music. Outside it's warm and summer, and I want nothing to do with it. I stay inside and keep to myself. The highlight of July is I go to the Hyundai dealership with my dad and I buy an Accent. The highlight of August is a very unexpected phone call.

CHAPTER 52

I'm sitting alone at a table in Perkins, drinking coffee and smoking a cigarette, waiting for my mom. She called the house about an hour ago, telling me she's in town and she wants to meet with me, so I showered and got into my new car and drove into the city. The last time I saw my mom was at my high school graduation.

I see her come through the front entrance. She says something to the hostess, then she sees me and smiles, and she waves and walks over. She's dressed like a businesswoman from the '80s. She sits.

"Hello, Brendan," she says.

"Hi, Mom," I say.

She waves at the air, at my smoke.

"You're smoking," she says.

"Yeah."

"I wish you wouldn't. It's so bad for you."

"I've heard that."

"So? How are you?" she asks.

Terrible, Mom. I lost my girlfriend and all of my friends and in a week I start college and I don't know if I can do it and I hate everything. I fucking hate everything.

"I'm surviving," I say.

"How's your dad?" she asks.

"He's good."

"He tells me you got a new car."

"Yeah."

"That's exciting."

"Sure."

"And you're starting school soon? That's exciting."

"Yeah."

The waitress comes to take my mom's order. She asks for coffee.

"You're not getting food?" I ask.

"No. I can't stay long. My flight's in a few hours. Did you get food?" my mom asks.

"Yeah. I ordered a burger and fries," I say. "Your flight back is today?"

"Yeah."

"How long have you been in Winnipeg?"

"Oh, a few days, I think. I was really busy. I was visiting your aunt and uncle."

"Oh."

"So, tell me about this course you're going to take," my mom says.

I'm silent. I stare down at my coffee as I snuff out my cigarette.

"Mom," I say, "can I come to Toronto with you?"

She laughs, then stops laughing when she sees I'm serious.

"Where's this coming from?" she asks.

"There's nothing here for me, Mom," I say. "I have nothing here and it's killing me. I want to leave. I want to go far away from here. I can start over in Toronto. I can be someone else. Please. I want to go there with you."

"But what about school?" she asks.

"Fuck school," I say.

The waitress comes and drops off my mom's coffee. She doesn't touch it.

"Brendan, your life is here with your dad and my life is there. That's just the way it is," she says.

I nod, still staring at my coffee. Neither of us speak for a moment. Mom looks at her watch.

"Well, I should get going. Don't want to miss my plane. This should cover the bill," she says, taking two twenties out of her purse and handing them to me.

She stands and kisses the top of my head.

"Everything will be okay," she says, then leaves.

My coffee cup is empty, so I take my mom's abandoned cup and I put cream and sugar in it and drink it. My burger and fries arrive, and I eat them by myself. The bill is $11.95. I leave my mom's twenties on the table, and I go home.

CHAPTER 53

It's Friday and I'm at the gas station, behind the counter. Chantelle is ... I don't know where the fuck she is. The store is empty when one of my favourite customers comes in. The old Irish woman walks slowly over to the part of the counter that has the lotto ticket machine. She smiles at me while she digs into her purse for scratch tickets for me to redeem. Her husband is nowhere to be found.

"I haven't seen you for a while," I say. "Where's your husband?"

She smiles again.

"Oh, he's no longer with us. He's in a better place," she says.

These two sentences absolutely destroy me.

When I can speak, I say, "Oh my god, I'm so sorry."

"It's okay. He went peacefully."

I redeem the woman's tickets. I'm completely incapable of thinking of anything else to say. After I give her her winnings, I manage, "Have a nice day."

She smiles again and makes her way to the door. "You, too."

The old Irish woman is gone when Chantelle appears from the back.

"I have to go to the bathroom," I tell her as I run past her.

I make sure to turn on the loud exhaust fan before I close the bathroom door. I lock it, then stand in the middle of the bathroom and cry. This isn't a few sniffles and a single tear rolling down my cheek. This is full-on, doubled-up sobbing, as violent as any bout of vomiting I've ever endured. I'm forcing pain and anger and despair out of my eyes. The sound coming out of me is that of a billy goat. I'm thankful for the exhaust fan, covering it all up.

It's not just that the old Irish man is dead, though that was the straw that broke my back. It's everything. It's the stuff with the guys, the stuff with Anne, with my mom, everything. And oh my Christ, I'm starting school next week. What if I can't do it? Anne coached me through the entrance process. What if I need her for everything else, too? I'm going to fail and have to drop out and I'll have no choice but to become a bricklayer.

Tears running down my face in a gas station bathroom, I can see the rest of my life, from this moment until they put me in the ground, and I don't like it.

No.

You're going to be a writer.

Like Anne said, it's your destiny.

Anne ...

I stop crying. I go to the sink and splash water in my face. I dry off with a paper towel and I get back to work.

On Sunday, I'm sitting at the kitchen table with my dad. We're eating barbecued steak and potatoes. It's quite good.

"You all ready for school tomorrow?" he asks.

"Yeah, Dad."

"I've sunk a lot of money into this, so you better kick ass," he says, smiling.

I smile too.

"I'll try, Dad."

"I make it a point not to pry into your personal life, Brendan, but I notice you're not really going out anymore, and you haven't brought your lady around since that one time," he says.

"What are you asking?"

"Are you and your lady still together?"

"No. Not for a while."

"Your choice or hers?"

"Mine."

"Well, that's stupid."

"You don't know what you're talking about."

"No?" my dad says. "I don't know about being alone? I'm the world heavyweight champion of being alone. I could write the book on being alone, boy. And you know what I learned too late?"

"What's that?"

"It's optional," he says.

"Dad, she cheated on her fiancé with me," I say.

He's thoughtful for a moment, chewing his steak.

"So she had a choice between you and at least one other guy, and she chose you?" he says.

"I can't condone that type of behaviour," I say.

"Sounds like your pride's hurt, son," my dad says. "The question you gotta ask yourself is this: Do you want to be a lonely, broken-down old man with your pride intact, or do you want to be with the woman you love? Take it from this broken-down old man. You want to be that other guy."

"Dad, I was cheated on once," I say. "It kinda really sucked. It was humiliating. Anne's fiancé, when she told him, probably felt exactly the same way. If I stayed with her, it would have been like saying what she did was okay.

It would be like saying what Marissa did to me was okay. It's not okay to do something like that to someone. It makes you not trust people."

My dad is looking at me with a smile on his face.

"What?"

"Do you not hear yourself?"

"Shut up."

"Don't let something that happened to you in your past ruin things for you now," he says. "That girl loves you. I saw it when you had her over here. A woman's love is a precious thing. You don't throw that away. I know that now. You don't throw that away because some little confused girl treated you bad one time. You learn from your mistakes; you don't repeat them. Boys repeat their mistakes. Men learn. Be a man."

My dad gets up from the table and places his dirty dishes in the sink. Then he leaves the kitchen. He leaves me to think about what he said. I finish my steak and potatoes only because they're so delicious, and then I'm putting my shoes on and I'm driving into the city. I park outside Anne's apartment. I sit in my car for a while. What am I doing? She could've moved. She could have a new boyfriend by now. She could be back with that Richard asshole.

Fuck it.

I go to the building entrance and I buzz Anne's apartment.

"Yes?"

"Anne, it's Brendan," I say.

Silence for a moment.

Then, "I'm coming down."

Waiting for her to come down to the entrance is the longest wait I've ever endured. She opens the door dressed in pajamas. She looks very tired.

"What do you want?" she says.

"I think I may have made a mistake," I say.

"What mistake was that?"

"Letting you go."

Silence. Anne is staring down at her slippers.

"You wanna come up and help me sleep?" she asks.

"Yes, I do," I say.

And I do.

CHAPTER 54

Anne has just come out of the shower. She's getting dressed. So am I.

"I didn't realize you start CreComm today," she says. "I hope you won't be too tired."

"I'll be fine," I say. "So, are we good?"

"How so?"

"Are we, like, back together and stuff?"

"That's up to you. Do you want to be back together?"

"Uh, yeah."

"Okay, then we're back together," she says.

I'm smiling at her.

"Just like that?" I ask.

"I never stopped loving you. You were the one who left. You're the one who ended things. If you want things to be back the way they were, then that's up to you. They never stopped being that way for me," Anne says.

Dressed now, she walks over and hugs me.

"I never meant to hurt you," she says. "I tend to make bad decisions."

"Well, now we'll make bad decisions together," I say.

"Sounds good," she says.

"Just one question, though."

"Shoot."

"Richard, that night at the restaurant, said, 'She's your mess now.' What did he mean by that?" I ask.

Anne is at the mirror on her dresser, doing up her hair.

"Richard had an idea of what a woman should be. He had an idea of how a woman should act. He hated vapid women. He held women to this impossible standard. It was a strange sort of misogyny. Anytime he learned anything about me that didn't fit into his perfect bubble of what a woman should be, he'd get upset. For example, he hated that I first had sex at fourteen. I could see it in his eyes sometimes when he looked at me. He saw me as broken or dirty. Real women didn't give it up so young. Real women were chaste and proper. Real women were princesses that you weren't ashamed to bring home to mama. To him, I was not that. I was a mess," she said.

"What a prick," I said.

"Yeah."

"But he asked you to marry him."

"Yeah."

"So he couldn't have been too repulsed by you."

"There's a pretty strong link between revulsion and attraction. The very things that repulsed him were what also attracted him to me. I got kinda fed up with his bullshit, so I moved out of his house and got this place. He was afraid of losing me, so he proposed, and I said yes mainly because I didn't have the heart to say no, and that's when I stopped sleeping. You pretty much know the rest from there," Anne said.

"I'm sorry I let an asshole like that come between us," I say.

"It's okay. It's all in the past now."

I drive Anne to work, and then I'm parking at the downtown Red River College campus. CreComm orientation is in the lunchroom on the fourth floor. I sit with seventy-four other new CreCommers and we listen to our instructors tell us a little about the different classes. Then some second-year students speak to us about what to expect from first year. Then the second-years are leading us out of the building and down the street to the King's Head Pub for beers. I get a pint of Alexander Keith's

India Pale Ale, because that seems like the proper beer to drink at an English pub. I sit at a table and acquaint myself with some of my peers. Everyone seems really nice. Everyone seems really impressed that we're spending our orientation day drinking and hanging out.

I don't make my lifelong friends that day. That takes time. Nothing's immediate. But it happens. Just as Anne promised it would.

About three weeks into the course, I head up to the fourth-floor lunchroom, appropriately, at lunchtime. I'm quite tired, so I find an empty round table and put my head down to nap. I wake up an indeterminate amount of time later to find that the empty round table I'm sitting at is no longer empty. I'm surrounded by guys from my class. They say hello to me and ask whether I had a nice nap.

And just like that, I have friends again.

That evening, I'm putting my shoes on at Anne's door. I'm grinning like an idiot.

"I really like the people in my class," I say.

Anne's smiling, too.

"Yeah? That's good."

"It's just like you said. It's a dating service for friends. Everyone's got the same interests and shit. It's awesome," I say.

"How's the work going?" Anne asks.

"Nothing I can't handle," I say. "We have our first real journalism assignment this week."

"Sweet."

I'm done tying my shoes. I stand up.

"This commute is killing me, though," I say. "Why does Oakbank have to be so far? Also, I can't come by tomorrow. I'm working the evening shift at the store."

Anne has a serious look on her face.

"Brendan, why don't you move in here?" she asks.

"For real?"

She smiles.

"Yeah. It makes sense. You're in the city for school every day. It just makes sense to live here as well. It's completely impractical for you to be still living in Oakbank. You're in the Exchange District for school, then you're here to see me, then you're back in Oakbank to sleep and work. You're all over the place, man," Anne says.

"That's the thing, though. I'd still have to go back to Oakbank for my shifts," I say.

Anne smiles again.

"Y'know, they have gas stations in the city, too," she says.

"You are correct," I say. "You really want me moved in here?"

"Absolutely. With you here every night, I could sleep every night."

"Plus, you could finally have your rent cut in half."

"Oh, fuck yeah."

We kiss and we decide that we'll discuss the matter further, and then I'm out the door and driving my long-ass commute home.

Thursday night, after school, I find myself at a nightclub on Pembina Highway watching people sing really poorly. *American Idol* is racking up viewers on TV, so this club is capitalizing on the craze. They're holding the first-ever Winnipeg Idol competition. The singing contest gets no marks for originality. People walk out onto the bar's stage one after the other and sing their hearts out in an attempt to win some fucking thing.

This is our first real journalism assignment. To cover the Winnipeg Idol karaoke contest. I suppose worse things have happened. Our first assignment could have been a school board meeting.

I'm standing, leaning against a pool table, notebook and pen in hand. James is beside me.

"What're you doing on Saturday?" he asks.

"No plans. What's up?"

"A few of us are going to the corn maze to hang out," James says.

A corn maze? Not a fucking bar, or a fucking nightclub, or some fucking idiot's house where we'll all sit around doing blow?

"That sounds awesome," I say.

"Yeah, man. Bring your lady, too, if you want," he says.

I'm smiling.

"I will."

Just then, a familiar face walks out on stage. It's one of the guys from our class. Without telling anyone, he signed up for the competition. The music starts and so does his singing, and I'm surprised to hear that he has a great voice, better than the other idiots in the competition. The CreCommers laugh and clap and sing along and cheer on our comrade.

CHAPTER 55

There are about one hundred of us. We're marching down Broadway, en route to the legislature building. Anne is beside me. She's holding a sign that says WAR ON TERROR = WAR WITHOUT END. I'm holding a sign that says NO WAR FOR EMPIRE.

We chant. We march. We wave our signs at passing cars. The drivers either look annoyed or laugh at us. It doesn't really deter us.

We pass cops who watch from the sidewalk, begging us with their eyes to step out of line. They want to use their Tasers and their pepper spray and their batons. We won't give them the satisfaction. This is a peaceful protest. You don't rail against violence with violence of your own.

If we smash windows and throw rocks and firebomb cars, then we're no better than the impotent old men who dispatch boys throughout the world to do their killing for them. Fuck them. This isn't a war. This is anti-war. This is peaceful civil disobedience.

It comes on slowly and by the time we reach the Leg, it's all I can think about. This is the kind of journalist I want to be. I want to be the guy on the ground, right in the thick of it, right in the shit of it. That's where the real story is. That's where the truth hides. I want to be there on the streets with the people when the bombs fall. I want to feel the shock wave. I want to smell the destruction. I want to be in the story. I want to write it from my first-hand perspective. I want to live the story.

The talking heads hovering above their tailored suits can have the safety and the security and the glory of the newsroom. The editorial columnist can sit and spew his misguided opinions in the comfort of his cubicle. I'll be on the streets, as I am now. Experiencing. And at night I'll open up my laptop and I'll put all those experiences to the page.

That's the kind of journalist I'll be.

I can't fucking wait.

CHAPTER 56

On Saturday, at the end of my shift, I walk into Jane's office and I quit. I'm not a dick about it. I thank her for giving me a job for so long and for putting up with my shit, and I tell her of course I'll work the next two weeks until she finds a replacement. She smiles and tells me that that's not necessary. I'm only working three shifts a week now because of school, so filling my spot on the schedule shouldn't be too hard.

She shakes my hand.

"Don't forget us little people when you're a big famous writer," she says.

I laugh.

"Being a famous writer is the closest thing you can come to being a regular person, in terms of fame. I'd have to be a real dick to get a big head because I'm a writer," I say.

"Well, just don't forget where you came from," Jane says.

"I won't."

I walk home, smoking cigarettes, smiling because this might be that last time I ever make this walk. Saturday evening, I pick up Anne and we hang out with my CreComm friends at the corn maze just outside of the city.

Sunday, I'm sitting in the middle of my bedroom, putting my shit into boxes. Anne's already got everything we need. She's got a bed, couch, entertainment unit, kitchen stuff, all that, so I'm boxing up only the CDs, movies, books and odd knickknacks that I want to move in with me.

My dad is standing in the doorway.

"I'll hang on to your bed and dresser in case you need them down the line," he says. "I'll put 'em out in the garage."

"What're you going to do with this room?" I ask.

"Think it's big enough to put a pool table in?"

"Probably not."

My dad smiles.

"I was thinking of turning it into a study," he says.

"I'll put the leather couch from the basement over there. I'll keep a little fridge for booze next to it and I'll put a big desk over here. I'll need a place to read all the books you're gonna write."

"Thanks, Dad."

He's silent a moment.

"That lady of yours —"

"Anne."

"— she's a good one. Don't fuck this up. Keep your eyes on the prize," he says.

I stand up.

"I will," I say.

We take the boxes out to my car and place them in the trunk and the backseat. My dad goes into the garage and comes out with two cartons of Export Gold.

"It might be a while before you get a new job. I don't want you to go without smokes," he says.

I laugh and take the cartons and throw them onto my passenger seat.

"Thanks, Dad," I say.

"I'm proud of you, kid," he says.

I just nod and shake his hand. Then I'm in my new car and gone.

My boxes are stacked up in Anne's living room. She said we'd deal with them later. Right now, we're seated on lawn chairs on her balcony, enjoying after-dinner cigarettes. There's an ashtray on top of a cooler in between us and I'm ashing into it, my legs stretched out and my feet resting on the railing in front of me. The sun has set behind a building to our right and the sky is on fire in orange and purple. The coolness of fall is no match for our hoodies.

I actually feel happy. It's new and weird and foreign and scary and really nice. I got so used to life being shit that it never occurred to me that it could be really great, too. And I know that this feeling won't last forever. Bad things happen to everyone, even happy people. But at least I have a taste for it now, and once you have a taste for something, you never forget. You hunger for it. You seek it out. You make it yours because it's precious to you. It's the light that banishes the darkness. From now on, I'm going to strive for happiness.

I guess I don't hate everything and everyone, after all.

Well ... let's not get carried away.

SEAN TRINDER grew up in a small town called Oakbank, located just outside of his current home of Winnipeg, Manitoba. A graduate of Red River College's Creative Communications program, he has worked as a news cameraman, an electrician's apprentice, and, yes, a gas station attendant. *The Guy Who Pumps Your Gas Hates You* is his first novel.